JUST SAYIN'

DANDI DALEY MACKALL

Tyndale House Publishers, Inc.
Carol Stream, Illinois

Visit Tyndale online at www.tyndale.com.

Visit Dandi Daley Mackall online at www.dandibooks.com.

TYNDALE and Tyndale's quill logo are registered trademarks of Tyndale House Publishers, Inc.

Designed by Jacqueline L. Núñez

Edited by Sarah Rubio

Scripture quotations are taken from the *Holy Bible*, New Living Translation, copyright © 1996, 2004, 2015 by Tyndale House Foundation. Used by permission of Tyndale House Publishers, Inc., Carol Stream, Illinois 60188. All rights reserved.

For manufacturing information regarding this product, please call 1-800-323-9400.

For information about special discounts for bulk purchases, please contact Tyndale House Publishers at csresponse@tyndale.com, or call 1-800-323-9400.

Library of Congress Cataloging-in-Publication Data

Names: Mackall, Dandi Daley, author.
Title: Just sayin' / Dandi Daley Mackall.
Other titles: Just saying
Description: Carol Stream, Illinois : Tyndale House Publishers, Inc., [2017]
Identifiers: LCCN 2016055489| ISBN 9781496423160 (hc) | ISBN 9781496423177 (sc)
Subjects: LCSH: Domestic fiction. | GSAFD: Christian fiction.
Classification: LCC PS3613.A27257 J87 2017 | DDC 813/.6—dc23 LC record available at https://lccn.loc.gov/2016055489

Printed in the United States of America

23	22	21	20	19	18	17
7	6	5	4	3	2	1

For Cassie and Ellie and Maddie
Just sayin' I love you guys!

Cassie Callahan
Hamilton, MO
June 8

Dear Mom,

Gram is making me write to you, even though it's past her bedtime (which is about three hours after she falls asleep in the recliner in front of the TV). She told me to tell you I'm doing great and that I understand why you need time alone to get over your broken engagement and your broken heart. But those are her words, not mine.

Think about it. Instead of living with you and Travis and one stepsister and one stepbrother, one of which is my age, I am living with a very old person. You know how Gram has always lied about her age? Well, she's started bragging about it now. I think that's how you know somebody's turning old, if you didn't have other things to go on, like wrinkles and the sappy black-and-white movies she watches and all the things she forgets. She's so old that when she went in to renew her driver's license, they said not only had her driver's license expired, but so had her birth date.

Also, old grandmothers don't get jokes. Like I told Gram if she would buy me a cell phone, I'd put her on speed dial and make her an InstaGRAM, and she told me to put a sock in it.

Kirby didn't eat for two days after you left. Poor dog. But I think she just misses Julie, not you. That dog (because she's seriously too big to call her a puppy anymore) has been sleeping on my bed. She chewed up one of Gram's slippers and Kittenie (my stuffed kitten, in case you forgot).

Since you've left me with Gram for who-knows-how-long, I thought you'd like to know what's really going on. Just sayin'.

Love,
Cassie

P.S. Do you know how to get blood out of denim? And sofa cushions? And the rug? And wood floors?

P.P.S. And kitchen tiles?

Callahan
el Norte Dr.
adino, CA 92404

Jennifer Callahan
San Bernardino, CA (temporarily)
June 12

Dear Cassie,

What did I tell you about getting a handle on your insults? When school starts up again, do you want to get suspended for name-calling . . . again? (Don't answer that.)

Please take it easy on Gram. I've left her with more responsibilities than she should have to handle. And by the way, your grandmother only acts old so that you'll do more around the house. She did the same thing when I was your age. She's probably younger than some of your friends' mothers.

I'm sorry I had to leave you with Gram, Cassie. I just need time to pull myself together. Travis and I would have been married one month from tomorrow if we hadn't gotten cold feet. I don't know if it would have worked out anyway. It probably wasn't really fair of me to ask you to share your room with little Julie. And you and Nick seemed to fight all the time, although I imagine real brothers and sisters the same age would fight too. But maybe it would have been too much for you to be handed an 11-year-old stepbrother and a 7-year-old stepsister just like that. So I guess it's all for the best.

Anyway, I don't suppose it matters now. All the same, I miss Travis, especially the way he couldn't stop smiling after he laughed at something—usually you and your insults. (But don't—I repeat, <u>do not</u>—take his laughter as encouragement for more insults. I know for a fact that Travis is as hard on Nick when it comes to banning insults as I try to be on you.)

Love you more than anything,
Mom

P.S. Tell Kirby not to sleep on your bed. She has a perfectly good bed of her own in the kitchen.

P.P.S. Cold water. I won't ask. And hey, don't you read my column in the <u>Hamiltonian</u> or the <u>St. Joseph Gazette</u>? I did a whole bit on how to get blood out of things.

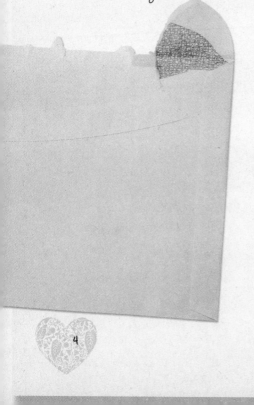

4

Cassie Callahan
Hamilton, MO
June 9

~~Dear Nick,~~ Hey, Camel Breath,

I can't believe you! Gram says you and Julie are going to a private school in the fall? I have no idea how she found out. And when I asked her, she narrowed her eyes to slits and said in a creepy voice, "I have my ways."

Really? A private school? What's that about? As if becoming city slickers isn't bad enough. What part of Chicago are you living in? You'd better keep cheering for the Royals, or else. And the Cardinals. Julie will let me know if you say anything nice about the Cubs or the White Sox, so don't get any ideas.

I miss your little sister. You'd better be nice to her, Nick—no insults. Got it? Julie is an insult-free zone.

I never had a chance to ask you something before you guys tore out of Hamilton, Missouri, like the town was on fire: Did you see this my-mom-and-your-dad breakup coming? I sure didn't. Otherwise, I wouldn't have gone through the agony of being fitted for that ridiculous bridesmaid dress, which Mom says I can wear to the prom in a few years. Right. If the prom will be held in Candy Land and my date is Lord Licorice or the Gingerbread Boy. Whatever you do, don't let Julie wear her bridesmaid dress to your fancy new school. Like kids need one more reason to pick on her.

I've been trying to be okay with the breakup, even though it wrecks all our plans. I thought about it all day yesterday when I walked by myself to the creek where you and I have found everything from fool's gold and arrowheads to raccoon skulls. The only "good" thing I could come up with about not having you as my stepbrother is that we won't have to be introduced as "steps." But since I couldn't sleep last night, here goes another try:

Top Five Reasons Why It's a Good Thing You Won't Be My Stepbrother:

5. You are a habit I'd like to kick ... with both feet.
4. You remind me of the ocean—you make me feel like puking.
3. You are garrulous, which means you talk too much. (Actually, I don't mind you talking so much if you don't mind me not listening so much.)
2. Your music. You have Van Gogh's ear for music. Even terrorists like the Beatles, C. B. (Camel Breath).
1. I tried very hard to come up with the #1 reason why it's a good thing that you won't be my stepbrother. I can't.

Your ex-almost-stepsister,
Cassie

P.S. Seriously, did your dad ever tell you why he broke off the engagement with my mom?

Nick Barton
Chicago, Illinois (only don't pronounce the S at
the end of ILLINOIS unless you want to really tick
people off)
June 13

~~Dear Cassie,~~ Hey, Amoeba Brain!

When are you going to get a phone, A. B.? In
case you haven't noticed, nobody writes letters
in this century. Ever hear of texting? I know
you hate talking on the phone because "half of a
conversation is being able to read the other guy's
expressions," blah blah blah. But if you had a cell,
you could text. And you'd see as many expressions
as you do in letters. Plus, you could use emojis—
not the smiley face, of course, but the one with
the tongue sticking out, or the frowning one.

City slickers? Garrulous? Seriously? I think
you've been hanging out with Gram too much—
you're starting to talk like an old person, even
more than usual, I mean. And are you still trying
to learn a new word every day? What is it with
you and words? Words are supposed to let people
know what you mean. Your words don't. I may talk
a lot, but at least it's in a language other kids
understand.

The private school wasn't my idea! Dad barely
speaks to Julie and me these days. He just mopes

around and grunts when you try to talk to him. And when he does talk, it's just to complain about Chicago traffic. I only found out about the school because he left the brochure on the counter. I yelled and screamed at him, but he wouldn't even talk about it. Julie, of course, just said, "I like the uniforms, Daddy."

My grandfather hired Dad to manage one of his waste disposal operations, the one on the north side of Chicago. We're staying in Grandad's old retirement condominium, so Julie and I are the youngest residents here by a century. Grandad's neighbor, a white-haired lady with a big smile that makes you smile when you look at her, calls Dad "young man." I think she has a crush on my grandfather, who has trouble remembering her name. And mine.

Grandad has a "housekeeper," who acts more like a "grandfather keeper." She stays with us during the day, and she's about 200 years old and almost totally deaf. Her hearing is as bad as Julie's is before Julie puts her hearing aids in. She reminds me of Ms. Ripples, the other fourth grade teacher, the one who looked like she'd break into pieces if anybody ran into her at recess.

Julie misses Kirby so much that she asked Dad for a dog or even a kitten. But the old-people place can't have pets—unless they're blind (the people, not the pets). Dad says he's looking for a house. He hates working for Grandad's business and being trapped in an office all day, but it was the only job he could get on such short notice. Besides, he has to take some kind of Illinois teacher's test and jump through some other hoops before they'll even let him teach here. Like 14 years teaching Missouri schoolkids isn't good enough?

Instead of a top-five list of why it's a good thing you're not my stepsister, I'm borrowing dialogue from Winston Churchill and Lady Astor (from last week's <u>The Hour of Insult</u>). I changed it a little:

Cassie: "If you were my stepbrother, I'd give you poison."
Nick: "If you were my stepsister, I'd drink it."

Your almost stepbrother,
Nick

P.S. I thought your mom was the one who broke off the engagement.

P.P.S. Go, Royals!

Cassie Callahan
Hamilton, Mo, still
June 16

Dear ~~Nick~~ Poshnick (Posh Private School Nick) (and FYI, POSH means "luxurious", and that means "fancy"),

Not only am I enjoying my quotidian practice of learning new words, but I am working on inventing a word so amazing that the dictionary people will put it in their official dictionary. I do not expect you to appreciate words the way I do. I'm just glad to see you stringing them together in sentences. Good for you, Poshnick!

Houston, we have a problem.

The one thing you and I have always agreed on is that Johnathan Kirby deserves the title of Insult King of the World, right? How many times have we sneaked into your basement to watch him insult his audience? And remember when your dad caught us watching the forbidden show and chased us out of the basement and we had to run uptown to watch the end of it through the window of Ray's TV and Appliance store? We stood outside in the rain listening to the King. At least with Mom gone, I can watch The Hour of Insult on Gram's TV. She's usually conked out in the recliner by then. Or she watches the show and calls it "vintage," which just means old-fashioned.

So, I wrote Kirby the King of Insults. I've written him two letters since you guys left Hamilton, and he

still hasn't answered me. They were nice letters too.
I signed your name with mine on the last letter, in case
he really means all those insults he gives to women on
<u>The Hour of Insult.</u>

What do you think about the word FABONOMOUS?
It would mean, of course, "enormously fabulous."

Me.
Cassie

Nick Barton
Chicago, IL, like it or not
June 19

Dear Cassie Knee-Skinner,

Watching Julie ride her bike around the old folks'
tiny condo courtyard this morning reminded me of
how many times you crashed your bike and skinned
your knees. Whenever I picture you (not that I do
this very much), you have Band-Aids on your knees.
You should see the old people at windows up and
down the condominiums, watching Julie ride her bike
(with training wheels). Something tells me nobody
has biked here for a long time.

In case you think I'm stupid, I figured out that
QUOTIDIAN means "every day," and I didn't even
look it up in the dictionary or online. So there.

The quotidian stuff Julie and I do at Grandad's
while Dad is at work is boring-er than mud.
Grandad tries to entertain us now and then.
Yesterday he asked us if we wanted to play Go
Fish. You know, the card game? When we said
we didn't, he took us to the aquarium, where we
watched fish swim for six hours. Six. Hours. Julie
dozed off and almost fell into the shark tank.

We've eaten takeout every night since we got
here. I know what you're thinking, but you're
wrong. I'm sick of takeout! What I wouldn't give
for a juicy burger fresh off the grill in your

backyard, or your mom's lasagna or spaghetti! I'd even eat your grandma's not-fried chicken and lumpy mashed potatoes. And maybe asparagus from your mom's garden.

Everybody always tells my dad that he looks just like his dad, my grandad. But I don't see it. I'll bet your mom thought my dad was handsome, and I doubt if she'd go for Grandad. I do get it when people tell me I look like Dad—dark hair, dark eyes, tallish, handsome. (Put smiley face here.) I guess my mom has dark hair too, but it's been so long since I've seen her that I could be wrong about that. Grandad said he heard that Mom's new husband (not James—she's got an even newer one) owns a shady or illegal factory in Dubai, which is so far away that even Grandad isn't sure where it is.

I'm not surprised that King Kirby hasn't answered your letters—your "nice" letters. What would the Insult King want with nice letters? That's not how to get his respect. He probably threw your letters into the garbage with the bouquet of roses they gave him after last year's season finale of The Hour of Insult. You better write him an insulting letter if you expect him to answer. And by the way, who gave you permission to sign my name?

Come on! FABONOMOUS? Back to the drawing board, if you ask me.

Signed by the real Nick

Cassie Callahan
Hamilton, MO
June 22

Dear Kirby, King of Insults,

I would be very angry with you if it weren't Be Kind to
Animals Week. Do you think I'm writing these letters
to you because my fingers need the exercise? Have
you bothered to answer even one of my letters? The
answer to both questions is no.

My almost-stepbrother says you're not fit to lick
my shoelaces. But I stuck up for you and said you were.
Now I'm thinking he was right all along, and that's not
a pleasant thought. He is quite garrulous and has a
quotidian habit of being wrong.

I saw you on the <u>Late Night Show</u> Tuesday night.
I liked your suit. Do you think it will ever come back
in style?

So, King, now you owe me three letters. (And I don't
mean A, B, C.)

Sincerely,
Cassie Callahan
And Nick

P.S. We have a dog, and we named her Kirby, in honor
of you. But if you don't "straighten up and fly right,"
as Gram would say, we're changing her name. The dog's,
not Gram's.

14

Johnathan Kirby, the Insult King
The Hour of Insult
New York, NY
June 26

Hey Kid,

Quit bothering me, will ya? You and that Nick guy!
Your letters are so bad it's a waste of time opening
them. Your letters are such a waste of paper that the
forestry department should lock you up for abusing
trees. I sure don't need you two kids to tell me I'm
the King of Insults. And the last thing I need is a
dumb dog named after me.

    Lick your shoelaces? My suit is out of style?
That the best you got, you amateurs? The King would
make mincemeat pie outta ya, if he had time to waste
on kids.

    The King don't like kids. They're just wrong.
Their heads are too big for their bodies, and their
hands and feet keep getting in their way and
breaking things. Not only should children never
be seen or heard, but they should never be read.
Stop writing, will ya?

    You're too much of a kid to know who W. C. Fields
was, but he was an actor who was pretty good at
insults. The most famous thing he ever said was,
"I never met a kid I liked." The King agrees
wholeheartedly.

Somewhere in the world, every five seconds,
a mother gives birth to a child. She must be found
and stopped!

Put a sock in it!
Kirby the King of Insults

Cassie Callahan
Still alone (except for Gram) (and Kirby)
in Hamilton, MO
June 29

Dear Know-It-All Nick,

I hate to admit it, but you were right about the Insult King. We (I signed your name too again) wrote him an insulting letter and got our very own insulting letter back! (Mom would not approve. But she's not here. And that's not my fault.) I will send you the letter later, since it's really to both of us. I want to show it to Pastor Mike first. But you need to write Kirby the King of Insults now. He asked you to. Kind of. If you read between the lines, where it's blank.

One thing you can insult him about is this: he closed the letter saying, "Put a sock in it." Bet you've heard Gram use that old line about a hundred million times! Plus, he insulted Kirby the Queen of Dogs.

Let me know if the King writes you back, okay? We can trade our letters from him.

Put a sock in it,
Cassie

P.S. Tell Julie I'm writing her, too.

Cassie Callahan
Hamilton, MO
June 29

Dear Julie,

Out of all the things lost when your dad dumped my mom, you're the one I miss the most. And feel free to tell your brother I said so. Is he being nice to you? Let me know if he gives you any trouble or any insults. You are not short. You are seven. So don't let Nick get away with calling you "Shorty."

In case Nick didn't tell you, Mom is giving herself some "alone time" to get over not marrying your dad. She's staying at her sister's in San Bernardino, even though Aunt Bev isn't there, because she's on a cruise with Uncle Benny somewhere in eastern Europe by now.

Mom is writing her columns from San Bernardino, and Gram says the newspaper doesn't even know the difference. Newspapers all across America are folding, but Mom's column about using Crisco to get rid of diaper rash, and the one about using crayons to repair scratches on your car, is getting picked up by every surviving paper and all the Internet versions.

Mom calls Gram every Sunday, Tuesday, and Thursday night, but I manage to be out of the house because hearing her voice can make me cry. (Do NOT tell Nick this.) And also, I hate the telephone, as you know. Only I wish I had a cell because then I could text you. I know that my mom misses you more than anything, Julie. She thought of you as the daughter she never had. Since I'm the daughter she DID have, that means I am pretty much chopped liver (as Gram would say).

Don't even get me started on Kirby. That dog whined for days after you left. She still curls up under your swing in our backyard and goes to sleep, probably dreaming of you. I had to let her start sleeping on my bed so she'd come inside the house at night. Even Gram felt sorry for her. Gram misses you almost as much as I do.

You should get your dad to read this to you if you can't make out some of the words, like "chopped liver" (which you can apply to a black eye for faster healing, says one of Mom's columns).

So, Travis, if you really are reading this, I guess you should know that I'm pretty mad at you for dumping us. Just sayin'.

Love (to you, Julie, but not so much to Travis anymore),

Cassie

Julie Barton
Chicago, IL
July 2

Dear Cassie,

I miss you!!!!!

   I wrote that by myself, but now I'm getting
Dad to write the rest because I want to say more
than just the words I know how to spell. Plus, it
was taking me way too long to try to write a whole
letter. So Dad is writing this for me, but I'm telling
him what to write.

   Besides missing YOU, here are other things I miss:

Your mom. She used to scratch my back to help me get
to sleep when you let me sleep over, and nobody else ever
did that.

Your backyard, and not just the playground stuff, but
you in it. And Nick in it too. I loved sitting on the swings
with you and not even swinging, but just talking about
stuff, like school and kids like Michael, who made fun of
the way I talked in kindergarten, or Kelsey, who called
me a baby because my bike has training wheels still and
hers doesn't. We were going to camp out in your backyard,
remember? And when Nick was there with us, he'd stand
by the swings while we were talking and swinging, and

he'd be tossing up his baseball and catching it in his mitt, so we had background music that sounded like WHUMP, WHUMP, WHUMP.

Kirby! I was afraid of dogs until you got that little black lab puppy. She was such a great puppy, and she loved me, didn't she? Do you think she'll forget me? How much has she grown? Maybe you should let her sleep on your bed, Cassie. Don't forget that she loves being scratched behind her ears.

I have 11 more things to list, but Daddy says he has to do some paperwork for his job, so this is the last one: I miss Daddy's and Nick's laughter. And even my own.

Love,
Julie

P.S. This is Travis now. It was your mom's decision to end our relationship, not mine.

Phone: *Ring! Ring!*

Gram: Hello?

Jen: Hi, Mom. Is Cassie home?

Gram: Of course not. She left on her bike and said she was going to youth group. I called Pastor Mike to make sure she got there. And I told him the only reason she's started going to youth group is that she doesn't want to talk to her mother. You ever thought about calling on a day when she doesn't know you're calling, Jen?

Jen: Yes.

[Long pause]

Gram: All right. That's what I thought.

Jen: What's Cassie been doing? Besides going to youth group?

Gram: That girl stays in her bedroom for hours and writes letters. I've been giving her postage money in exchange for having her do little jobs around here. You know what she did? She fixed the leaky faucet in the downstairs bathroom. And she got that old clock of your daddy's running again.

Jen: She's always been so good with things like that. Is she having friends come over? Or going to their houses? Or going swimming with anybody?

Gram: Nope. I think she misses Nick and Julie a lot more than she lets on. *[Pause.]* And she misses you. When are you coming home, Jennifer?

Jen: I don't know, Mom. I have to get to where I'm not crying all the time. I wasn't doing anyone any good when everything kept reminding me of . . . him.

Gram (*softer*): Are you ever going to tell me what that man did to make you run off like that?

Jen: . . .

Gram: All right.

Jen: Thanks for taking care of things there, Mom. Tell Cassie I'm sorry I missed her. But I'm glad she's going to youth group—even if it's just to get away from me. Tell her to go easy on Pastor Mike. Bye, Mom.

Gram: Bye yourself, honey.

Cassie Callahan
Hamilton, MO
July 2

Dear Pastor Mike,

I have to tell you that I still don't get it. I stopped asking you my question (about parents who break promises) in youth group tonight because I could tell you didn't want to answer me anymore. You wanted to talk about other (kinda boring) stuff. But that doesn't mean I accept the quick and easy answer you gave the group. I'm sorry if I insulted you by calling you "God's Mouthpiece," but the name doesn't sound like a bad thing to me, and I don't know why kids laughed. I didn't.

You probably figured out which parent and which promise I was talking about. You said a promise is like a contract, right? So WHY can't you make my mom live up to her contract? She and Travis booked the church and even gave you a down payment, right? They promised they'd get married, and that you would marry them, didn't they? So how come you let them off the hook?

A couple of months ago when you were giving a sermon about swearing (but I'm not sure that was what you were really talking about because Nick was sitting next to me, and he kept writing funny notes on the church bulletin), you read a verse that said, "Let your yes be yes and your no be no." Well, they said YES, and I don't think they should be able to say no now. You're the boss of church, aren't you? So don't let them get away with this!

Isn't there something in the Bible about parents taking care of their children? You might be interested to know that my mother has left me in the care of my grandmother, who is way too old to take care of me. "How old is Gram?" you ask. I'm pretty sure Gram was a waitress at the Last Supper.

I'm just sayin'.

Yours respectfully,
Cassie Callahan

P.S. What did you really think of my letter from Kirby, King of Insults? You looked like you were trying to hold in a laugh. Or maybe that green Kool-Aid got to your stomach like it did mine.

Nick Barton
Old People's Home
Chicago, IL
July 1

Dear Kirby the Insult King,

This is the first letter you're getting from me, although I'm the one who told Cassie she'd have to insult you to get you to write her back. She signed my name on her letters without my permission, by the way. I could sue her, but she's going through a lot now, so I won't. YOU would, I'll bet.

I guess you finally wrote her. I haven't seen that letter because Cassie and I aren't in the same place anymore. She's back in Missouri, where my dad and my sister and I were supposed to live after Dad married Cassie's mom. Only her mom dumped us and broke off the engagement, and so we're stuck in Illinois in an old folks' retirement home, where I can't even play my music without headphones on.

Cassie said you wrote back and said, "Put a sock in it," and that makes me wonder if you really are the King of Insults, because Cassie's grandmother says that all the time. And it isn't even funny or much of an insult, when you think about it. Every kid in my old class—except maybe Angela Brigmon—could come up with better insults than socks.

You also didn't express proper appreciation for the fact that we named what was supposed to be OUR dog after you. You should be honored. Kirby is a really fabonomous dog.

You may have heard that Miss Cassie Callahan's birthday is next month. She will be 11 years old, which I already am. You should send her a birthday present to cheer her up. And to make up for what you said about the dog.

Do it!
Nick

P.S. Did you really write "Put a sock in it!"?

Johnathan Kirby, the Insult King of the World
New York, NY, of course
July 5

Hey you! Kid Nick,

Don't yell at me! I'm not your mother!

I tried to read your letter, but I fell asleep
during the bit about poor you having to move to
Chicago. Boo hoo.

As for "Put a sock in it," that phrase, for your
information, kid, is a time-honored put-down.
Your ex-stepsister's granny sounds like the only
potential person in your messed-up families. Cry
me a river. You want to know about family? My
mother shot my father with a bow and arrow instead
of a rifle so she wouldn't wake us up. Now that's
a thoughtful woman for you! I always wanted a
stepmother. So I asked my mother to sit on the front
step for the rest of her life. It wasn't all it was
cracked up to be. Whaddaya want from me, anyways?

Were you two friends before you were getting to
be steps? Sounds like both of yous are the kind of
kids other parents tell their kids not to play with.

Why is your ex-stepsister needing to be cheered
up? Kids still like birthdays, don't they? But okay.
I'll send her several mouth-sized socks.

Go away now,
The King

Cassie Callahan
Hamilton, MO
July 11

Dear King,

Nick says you wrote him back. I haven't seen the letter
yet. I sent him the one you wrote me, but he forgot to
send me yours. Instead, he just copied parts of your
letter into his, "the parts that don't stink too much."

Right off, you made a big mistake. You wrote, "I'm
not your mother!" Nick's actual mother ran off when
Julie (Nick's sister) wasn't even one year old, and Nick
was only four-going-on-five. She divorced Nick's dad,
Travis, and married an old rich guy, then dumped HIM
for another rich guy who owns factories that break
the laws in countries like Venezuela and South Africa
and maybe Saudi Arabia. Gram told me Nick's mother
has a palace in a city called Dubai, which is pronounced
Do-Buy, and she does buy, like everything she wants.
But she never sends a nickel to Nick or a jewel to
Julie. Travis raised Nick and Julie all by himself. And
even though I'm still mad at him for dumping my mom
and me, I have to admit he did a pretty good job
raising them.

Nick said you asked why I'm not happy and not
looking forward to my birthday. And that is because
my mom probably won't be here for it. She isn't
here for anything. She's gone off to California to

"find herself," says Gram. But Mom's never been to California before, so I don't know why she'd be looking there. I haven't talked to her since she left. I don't have a cell phone. If she were here, I'd nag her for one. Nick said you're going to send me a couple of gifts for my birthday, and a phone would be a really great one. I already have your book of insults, so don't send that. It wasn't as funny as you are.

Nick says you said nice things about Gram, but that's only because you don't know her. Ellie's grandmother (a school friend, my best friend until she got a different best friend the first week of summer, when I didn't care so much, because I had Nick and Julie) has a thousand pictures of Ellie, her granddaughter, in her wallet and a million on her phone, including a video of her being born, which is kind of disgusting. Ellie's grandmother shows these pictures to everybody who can't get away fast enough. The mail lady's seen every picture a dozen times, and the grocery store checkout person has to stop her before she pulls out her phone pictures and clogs up the checkout line. My gram has two pictures of me, which I gave her myself, and which she couldn't find if her life depended on it, because she has so much junk everywhere.

It won't be my birthday until the end of summer, but you can go ahead and send the gifts to cheer me up if you'd like to. I won't open them until my birthday. Maybe.

Cassie, the Princess of Sad

Johnathan Kirby, the Insult King
Athens, PA
July 15

Dear Sad,

Well, boo hoo to you, too. Your gram sounds like
an okay gal. So what if she's not the fuzzy kind
of grandma who goes around showing everybody
pictures of her granddaughter? Do you go around
showing everyone pictures of your gram?

And big deal that your mom had to go to
California to get some time to herself. If you'd run
away from home like a normal kid, your ma wouldn't
have had to. Ever think of that?

How'd you like to be stuck in this Podunk town
that ain't even a town, but a borough barely outside
of New York State? Athens, Pennsylvania. Right.
If you've ever been to the real Athens in Greece,
let me tell you, this one ain't it. But try to tell
my dumbhead producer that. He's the one who came
up with the big idea to take my show on the road,
live, this season. Last week he wanted to shoot the
show from Athens, Ohio. Then he changed his mind,
considered Macedonia, then settled on Toronto,
Ohio. The guy is so loony that I caught him staring
at orange juice for 20 minutes . . . just because it
said "concentrate" on the carton.

I gotta start getting ready for a network meeting about my big live show, <u>The Last Insult Standing</u>. That's what comes after we do these shows in all the fake-sounding towns across America.

I'm busy now, kid. I'll ignore you some other time.

The King

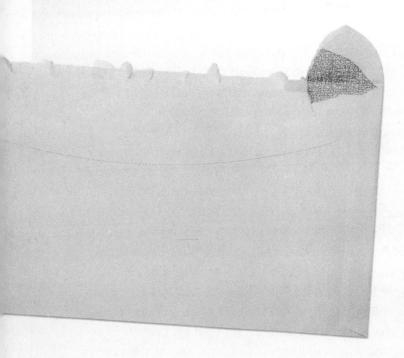

PASTOR MIKE
HAMILTON, MO
JULY 12

Dear Cassie,

I'm very happy you've started coming to youth group (even if it is only to get away from your mom's phone call). I wish Nick and Julie could come too. I really miss them.

Thank you for your letter. You're right—"God's Mouthpiece" is a great thing to be, and I only hope I can live up to the name. But the truth is, the Bible is God's real mouthpiece. We even call it the Word. And your grandmother tells me that you are crazy about words and are memorizing from your Word-a-Day calendar. Very impressive. Also very important to choose words wisely.

I'm sorry that your mother and Travis couldn't come together and go through with their wedding plans. As you know, I met with them several times, and I felt they were well suited for each other. Both share a genuine faith. I was as surprised as you to receive word of the cancellation. I tried to reach out to both of them but haven't heard back yet. As for enforcing their "contract," I'm sure you can see where that plan would eventually fail, even if I could enforce the commitment. A husband and wife must be dedicated to one another. And in this case, which involves two families, it's even more crucial to be of one mind.

I'm sorry I couldn't answer all your questions in youth group. Please feel free to ask me anything, even if you don't like my answers. And you are welcome to write me again. For a couple of Sundays, I have received notes from an anonymous sender via our offering plate. Our elders have found the critiques on the sermon and its length and even the song selection most amusing. You wouldn't know anything about that, would you?

Your grandmother tells me you've been spending a good deal of time in your room writing letters. Again, I will always welcome a letter from you and will do my best to answer it. But I wonder if you have ever tried writing to God. I think you might find better answers than merely writing to "God's Mouthpiece."

As for the unusual letter from Mr. Kirby, I guess I don't know what to think. I haven't watched his show, <u>The Hour of Insult</u>. I am surprised your mother allows you to watch it. Perhaps I'll tune in this week.

See you Sunday!
Pastor Mike

Nick Barton
Chi-Town, IL
July 13

Hey, Fruit Loops!

Why don't you get an e-mail address and use your gram's computer? I can't believe people used to only write letters like this. No texts. No e-mail. No social media. No phone. Just scratches on the cave walls.

I reread your letter from the King of Insults. I guess it's good he's writing us back, even though it does sound like he's siding with the adults against the kids. I saw an ad about a contest put on by The Hour of Insult. It's called The Last Insult Standing. Have you heard anything about it? Make the King fill you in.

Did you notice how the Insult King always sticks his stamps on upside down?

Julie and I visited our new school yesterday, and it was kind of creepy. There were a bunch of kids there going to school, even though it's still summer. They didn't even have to be there. I asked a couple of kids. They said they wanted to take an extra math course or get a head start on French. All the girls looked the same: same smile, same hair, same clothes. I didn't see a single skinned knee, so you definitely would have stood out.

I don't know how good the school is going to be for Julie, either. The principal kept bending down to talk to her. She'd get right in Julie's face and shout, even though she could see the hearing aids and should have known already about her kidneys and hearing and speech and stuff. Plus, the principal kept saying words like "gifted" and "special" and "exceptional" students, when she meant the ones who have trouble, like Julie. Dad said I need to give the whole thing a chance and that this isn't easy on any of us.

He got that right.

So you're even getting the pastor in on your letter writing? Pastor Mike's okay. Remember when we played flag football and I forgot about the flag part and tackled him and gave him a bloody nose? He didn't even get mad. He's probably onto something when he tells you to write to God. I vote you give it a shot. Why not write God, as long as you're writing everybody else? Only I still say you should try e-mailing.

Wish you were here—or we were there!

Signed,
Nick the Nice
(Julie said you commanded me to be nice.
And since you're corresponding with God now, I
thought it wouldn't hurt for you to think of me as
Nick the Nice.)

P.S. Tell God I said hi. And would he He mind getting us out of that private school? If He can get all those Israelite children out of Egypt, getting Julie and me out of that school should be a snap.

Cassie Callahan
Hamilton, MO
July 15

~~Dear God,~~

~~Thou probably already knoweth all about me, so I won't~~
~~wasteth your time telling you about me since you~~
~~knowest me inside out. And that means Thou knowest~~
~~whateth I am about to sayeth even before I sayeth it.~~
~~And no matter what I sayeth, Thou knowest better and~~
~~knoweth what I really meaneth.~~

Dear Jesus,

I've been sitting on my bed and trying to write your
Father (and mine), and it just hasn't been working for
me. Then I got the bright idea of writing to you. You've
been down here on earth, not exactly in Missouri, but
close enough. So I figure you probably get it.

Things can get pretty crazy down here, as you
know. You went without your real Father for a while,
and even the stepfather you had down here, Joseph,
kind of faded out of the picture early on, and Pastor
Mike (you know him—he's the one who suggested I write
to you) told us that Joseph probably died before you
got really famous.

Anyway, I'm not sure how this works, but I know you
guys are Father and Son and also only one God, with
the Holy Spirit thrown in. So I don't think God or the

37

Holy Spirit will mind or get jealous or anything because, well, you're all one anyway.

I know I should be writing you a thank-you letter for giving me a good home and life and health and a mother and a grandmother. So, thank you. But you probably already know that's not the real reason I'm writing. I am not very happy with the way this almost-marriage thing turned out. Not at all happy about that. I really wanted Travis as a stepdad. I thought he liked me enough to make me his stepdaughter. At first, I felt guilty for wanting that, like I was betraying my real dad. But to tell you the truth, I can barely remember my real dad. Mostly, I know what he looks like from pictures (he's always laughing and so am I). And I think I remember his voice, because sometimes I hear a man's voice, and I have to look quick because it sounds like his. Only it's not. I know it wasn't his fault that he died in the accident, and Mom said it happened so fast that he probably didn't even know what hit him. (It was a truck that couldn't stop on the ice, but you knew that.) And I don't like that it happened, but things like that do happen down here, as you know.

I've been praying that Travis and Mom would get back together, but it doesn't look like that's going to happen. I know I should have prayed more while they were together, right? But if there's anything you can do, I'd sure appreciate it.

Thanks again.

Yours truly,
Cassie (the one in Hamilton, Missouri)

P.S. I just remembered that I should capitalize "you." And I didn't do that. And if I go back and change the Ys, this letter will be messier than it already is. So please don't read anything into the small y. I don't mean anything by it. Thanks.

P.P.S. Nick says to tell you hi and could you please get him and Julie out of that private school. And Nick forgot to capitalize "you" also, but he doesn't mean anything by it either.

Cassie Callahan
Hamilton, MO
July 15

Hey, Lumphead,

Don't you think I would e-mail if I could? I do like writing
letters more than you do, I admit. I can write when I'm
plopped on my bed, or when I'm watching a boring show
of Gram's on TV, or while I'm eating, or even while I'm
in church. But Gram won't let me near her computer.
She still hasn't forgotten about all the freebie sites I
subscribed to on her old computer and how she had to
shut down her e-mail and the whole account because
of all the junk mail she got after that. For an old
person, she sure has a long memory.

    I wrote to God. Then I crossed out the letter
because it sounded fake, and I wrote to Jesus. It was
not a thank-you letter. I didn't mail it or anything, with
"Heaven" as an address. He's not Santa Claus. I used to
write Santa c/o the North Pole. Once, he wrote back
and said I'd been a good girl, so I figured he didn't
really see me when I was awake.

    I will let you know if I hear back from God.
Or Jesus.

    Landri and Hannah invited me to their birthday
parties, but I'm not going, because I don't think I'm
going to get to have a birthday party of my own this
year, and it wouldn't be fair to go to theirs. Hannah

is doing the bounce house party at the Y again—been there, done that. But Landri is having a roller skating and pizza party, so I wish I could go.

Oh well.

Bye,
Cassie
and by Cassie (Get it?)

P.S. I didn't use my word for the day today. It's JUBILANT, and it means "really happy," and I couldn't think of a single sentence for it.

P.P.S. I feel so miserable not having you here, Nick. It's almost like having you here.

Cassie Callahan
Hamilton, MO
July 15

Dear Pastor Mike,

I did it. I wrote to God like you said. I didn't know where to mail it, so I biked to church and slid it under the front door. If God hasn't picked it up, you might find it there yourself. And that's fine because if God can see inside me, I don't think He'll have any trouble seeing inside the envelope.

Actually, I had trouble writing to God, so I just wrote to Jesus. I know you said they're the same Person, with the Holy Spirit, too, and you should probably go over that one again because it's pretty confusing. But writing Jesus came easy, although I complained a lot and asked for something he already said no to.

I wish Jesus would write me back. Yes, I know that's not how it works. But wouldn't it be cool if it did? If I checked the mailbox and found a letter from Jesus Christ, Heaven?

On the other hand, I might not like everything Jesus would write in that letter. Mom used to give Nick and me a "Silver Rule." Instead of "Do unto others as you would have them do unto you," she'd make it: "SAY to others what you'd want them to say to you." Nick and I have insulted each other so much, the insults are kind of automatic.

I know Jesus is busy with wars and famine and plagues and everything, including the yahoos (as Gram calls them) running for president of the United States. But it sure would be great if he could take some time out to write me. Maybe you could ask him next time you pray.

See you Sunday!
Cassie

PASTOR MIKE
HAMILTON, MO
JULY 16

Dear Cassie,

Thanks for letting me know that you wrote to Jesus. Don't worry about complaining too much. And you shouldn't feel bad about asking for something you want, even if you asked before and didn't get it.

You're wrong about Jesus not writing you back, though. Why do you think we call the Bible "the Word of God"? That's God/Jesus writing you, Cassie. And many of the "books" of the New Testament are actually letters passed around among churches—like the letter to the Galatians, to the Ephesians, to the Colossians, and to the Romans. Pull out that Bible you got when you joined youth group and check out these verses (hint: look in the front, the table of contents, to get the page numbers for the books):

> Matthew 7:7
> Lamentations 2:19

See you Sunday,
Pastor Mike

P.S. If you come to youth group tonight, I'll give this to you then.

Cassie Callahan
Hamilton, MO
July 17

Dear Private Nick,

This will be short because it's really your turn to write me. And it's my turn to write Kirby, King of Insults. But I promised to let you know if I heard back from God. I have. Kind of. Pastor Mike says the Bible is a bunch of letters to us. At youth group last night, he tried to explain that even though people like Matthew and Moses and Paul wrote the words, God was behind the writing. The Holy Spirit got in on it too. So anyway, that's how I heard back from God, especially about complaining to him and asking something he already said no to, and I'm pretty sure you know what I asked and didn't get an answer to, because you guys are in Chicago and I am still in Hamilton.

    Matthew 7:7: "Keep on asking, and you will receive what you ask for. Keep on seeking, and you will find. Keep on knocking, and the door will be opened to you."

    Lamentations 2:19: "Rise during the night and cry out. Pour out your hearts like water to the Lord."

    I think those are pretty good answers. I've done a lot of crying out in the night and pouring out my heart lately, although as you know, I'm no crybaby.

I'm going to write Jesus again, and I'm going to keep complaining and asking for stuff. Only I'll throw in more thank-yous and way-to-gos.

Yours,
Cassie the Complainer

P.S. And I didn't forget to bring up the private school problem.

P.P.S. Jesus is not a prestidigitator, so you should keep asking him yourself.

P.P.P.S. PRESTIDIGITATOR, my word for the day, means "magician."

Cassie Callahan
Hamilton, MO
July 17

Dear King of Insults,

Stop siding with my grandmother, will you? I'm telling you,
you are only sticking up for Gram because you don't
know her. She is very bossy. She doesn't do insults, but
sometimes she laughs when Nick insults me (or when he
used to). I'm almost the shortest kid in my class, if you
don't count Adam, who's a year younger than the rest
of us because he's really smart. Nick was always saying
stuff like:
   "Go play with your buddies, the Keebler elves."
   "You're bored? Why don't you sit on the sidewalk and
swing your legs?"
   "Go surf on a Popsicle stick."
   Gram did try (not very well) to hide her laughter at
my expense. She'd cover her mouth, but her shoulders
shook. She and Mom claim to hate insults, which is why
Nick and I are forced to watch your show when they're
not looking.
   Plus, Gram must really want to get rid of me. She's
been trying hard to get me to go to Ellie's sleepover.
I told her I didn't have a sleeping bag. She said, "So
what? You can use my quilt." (Like it wouldn't be total
humiliation to show up for a sleepover armed with your
grandmother's quilt?) But the truth is I'm never going

47

to sleep over at anybody's house or go to Landri's birthday party, even though I got invited and would really like to go.

Julie, my almost-stepsister, Nick's sister, is seriously little for her age because she has nephritis, which means kidney disease in case you didn't know that word. Gram would trade me in for Julie in a heartbeat, and I can't blame her for that, because I'd trade Gram for Julie too.

There isn't much to write you about since Julie and Nick are gone and I'm stuck here with my pushy grandmother. But I wrote a letter to God, well, to Jesus really. And he sort of wrote back. And I'm pretty sure I'm going to write him back. You should write him sometime yourself.

Enchantingly yours,
Cassie

P.S. Hey! Are you changing TV shows or something? What's <u>The Last Insult Standing</u>?

Johnathan Kirby, the Insult King of the World
Currently in Bethlehem, PA (and hating this road
trip and the producer who scheduled it)
July 20

Kid Callahan,

Why in heaven's name would I write to Jesus? I'm the
King of Insults. So you want I should insult God or
something? And how do you know I'm not Jewish?
    And anyhow, I don't need him. I'm a self-made man.
    Why aren't you going to parties if you're invited
and want to go?
    Why are you still writing me? Does it make you
feel important to be writing somebody famous?

Go away!
The King

P.S. The more I hear about Gram, the luckier I think
you are to have her. Her, not so much.

Cassie Callahan
Hamilton, MO (but I'd love to be on a road trip
to Athens or Bethlehem)
July 22

Dear So-called King,

You can't really believe that I'm writing you because
YOU'RE famous and important. I write to God! And
Jesus!

   Plus, you only think you're self-made. Where did you
get your bones and flesh and blood and guts (such as
they are)? Who cares if you're Jewish or not? So was
Jesus. Duh.

   You would probably enjoy exchanging letters with
Jesus. In fact, Jesus is much better at insults than you
will ever be. Here's how he took down the Pharisees,
the big shots who thought they were self-made,
famous, and important:

   Blind guides! You strain your water so you won't
   accidentally swallow a gnat, but you swallow a camel!
   . . . Hypocrites! For you are so careful to clean
   the outside of the cup and the dish, but inside you
   are filthy—full of greed and self-indulgence! . . .
   Hypocrites! For you are like whitewashed tombs—
   beautiful on the outside but filled on the inside with
   dead people's bones and all sorts of impurity. . . .
   Snakes! Sons of vipers!

(That's all in Matthew 23, in case you think I'm making this stuff up.)

So there!
Cassie

P.S. You forgot to tell me about <u>The Last Insult Standing</u>. You old folks are always forgetting important stuff. Sigh . . .

Johnathan Kirby, King of Insults (no so-called
about it)
Prague, NE (but they pronounce it PRAYG)
July 25

Dear Cassie,

Okay. I admit it. Not bad. I especially loved the
"whitewashed tombs" and "sons of vipers." Think
Jesus would mind if I used those in my act?

Speaking of my act, I'll tell you about my big
show, but I'm only doing it to get you off my back. If
you ain't been living underground, you know that
my regular show, The Hour of Insult, has taken to
the road this year. We've filmed our shows all over,
from Moscow, Idaho; to London, Kentucky; to Berlin
(called BERlin), New Hampshire; to Dublin, Texas;
and beyond. Even Wales and Fishhook, Alaska, where
it was so easy to insult people it was hardly worth
the effort.

For our season finale, we'll be doing the show
live from middle America, in Hannibal, Missouri,
birthplace and hometown of Mark Twain, who
was the Insult King of his day and also not a bad
storyteller. Instead of my usual Hour of Insult,
we're running a two-hour live contest with regular
joes and calling it The Last Insult Standing.

If you want to know more than that, tough. You
can tune in to my show this week and listen up so

as you can learn how the whole thing works. I got people who do that kind of detail boring stuff for me so I don't got to.

Now leave me alone.

The King

P.S. Say hello to your grandmother for me.

Emma Mae Hendren (Gram)
Hamilton, MO
July 20

Dear Mr. Kirby:

I am writing to ask you straight-out if you are some kind of crook, con man, or predator. I am nobody's fool, and I know you have been corresponding with my almost 11-year-old granddaughter, Cassie Callahan. I see those letters lying around. What am I supposed to do? Let them be? No creep is going to reach my granddaughter through the US mail (or any other method, like on the Internet, where I will not allow her to go)—not on my watch, mister. And this is my watch, since my daughter left me in charge while she licks her wounds in California.

So I read your letters. And you'll get no apology from me. It's my duty.

And now I have a few things to say.

You were pretty insulting to Cassie, but I guess that's to be expected, given your chosen profession. And although I didn't get a chance to read Cassie's letters to you, my guess is that the kid gave as good as she got, in spite of the best efforts of her mother and me to get her to stop with the insults already. Cassie might even have sent you to the dictionary, with her vocabulary as big as it is and growing every day. Yesterday she said she'd write her mother, but it would be a laconic reply because of her mom's dilatory tactics. I didn't have time to hunt in a dictionary, so I just said, "Do it!"

If you are not a predator, then I feel it incumbent (one of Cassie's words from last week) upon me to thank you for your support. It's not easy trying to help my daughter and my granddaughter. I'm not complaining, but this whole breakup sent my daughter Jen into a tailspin. She never did tell me why Travis left. The wedding was all arranged, and she was even going to wear my wedding dress. My husband died in the Vietnam War, and Jen's husband, Cassie's father, was killed in a car accident when Cassie was just two years old. We do not have good luck with husbands in our family, so maybe it's for the best that Travis got out while he could.

Still, I wish Jen and Travis could have made it. Instead, Cassie is stuck with me, and it's only fair to say that I am not your usual sweet granny. I don't believe I'm a grouch, but I'm old. How old? Well, you could tell by counting the rings under my eyes. My husband always remembered my age but forgot my birthday.

If you are a predator, stop writing my granddaughter. If you're not a predator, have a nice day.

Sincerely,
Emma Mae Hendren, aka Gram

Johnathan Kirby, the King of Insults
Manila, UT
July 25

Dear Emma Mae/Gram,

No, I'm not a crook, con man, or predator. Of course,
I suppose if I were, I wouldn't tell you. Anyway,
your granddaughter started this whole letter thing.
I didn't even write her back until the third letter,
when she started calling me names that would have
done a sailor proud. I'll bet it's not smooth sailing
through school for that one. Doesn't strike me as
the teacher's pet.

I am sorry to hear about your husband and Jen's
husband.

So what's up with this Travis guy? Did he cheat
on your daughter or something? Hard to believe
he's too horrible since Cassie misses him so much. I
even heard from the guy's son, Nick. I think he's as
bummed as Cassie. And what's up with the other one,
the little sister? Judy? Julie? Something like that.

There are worse things than being old—like not
getting to be old, right? You hear people talking
about their "old friends" or their "old buddies."
I've always wondered what that would be like.
I never stayed in one place long enough to make
friends. Or maybe I just don't know how. And now I'm
old, without old friends. How old? Well, I wouldn't

be so old if I hadn't been born so long ago. My first
pet came straight off Noah's ark. When I was a kid,
the Dead Sea was just starting to get sick.

On television they make me wear makeup so I won't
look so old. And they have special camera lenses
to blur some of the wrinkles, although this high-
definition television is a curse. My dermatologist
doesn't even make me come into the office to examine
my face for cancer spots. He just watches the show.

Definitely not a crook,

The King

(but you can call me Kirby, an old friend)

P.S. I think Cassie should go to her friends' parties,
don't you?

Cassie Callahan
Lonesome in Hamilton, MO
July 24

Dear Mom,

I'm sorry about missing your phone call. Again. I was in youth group, where Pastor Mike was trying to tell us the difference between good advice and bad advice. But I pointed out that if we know the difference between good advice and bad advice, we don't really need advice.

I probably talk too much in there, but Pastor Mike doesn't make me feel like it, and I'm trying hard to only say nice things to the other kids. Pastor Mike has been talking to us about "wholesome" speech, and you know how I like learning about words. But this was a new thing—wholesome, like healthy. Healthy words. He passed out bookmarks with Proverbs 12:18 on them: "Some people make cutting remarks, but the words of the wise bring healing."

I could use some of that healing.

I admit that I walked back home very languidly so that you and Gram would be finished talking before I got there. It's not that I'm mad at you or trying to punish you, like Gram thinks. I just don't want to get all sad all over again. Or say something I'll feel bad about later. Something not wholesome or healing. Then you'd feel worse. And so would I. Plus, you already know I hate the phone. Maybe if you bought me a cell phone, though, I would learn to like it. And in the meantime, I could text.

I think Gram has been reading my mail. Please tell her that's against the law. And don't you think she should let me use her laptop? I would write you more often if I could e-mail.

Three people at church asked me about the "upcoming wedding." You'd think gossip would get around faster in a town as small as this. I told them I didn't know what they were talking about. And the truth is, I don't.

Come home.

Love,
Cassie

P.S. Did you know that Travis is making Nick and Julie go to this private school, where everybody has to dress, talk, and think the same? It sounds very scary and wrong to me. Don't be surprised if Nick runs away from home and joins the Marines.

Nick Barton
Chicago, IL
July 23

Dear Gorilla Breath,

I know it's my turn to write, and I've been trying.
But Dad is ruining my life. He's impossible to please.
If he were a dog, he'd be growling all the time
and biting sometimes too. He even snaps at Julie.
I think it's your mom's fault. You need to write her
(because I know you and your phone phobia) and
make her tell you why she dumped my dad the
way she did. What did she do or say to him to
make him turn into a grump?

Desperate (one of your words) in Chicago,
Nick

P.S. I like Jesus' answers. Are you going to write
him again? If you do, ask him to turn Dad back into
a normal guy. And keep mentioning the private
school.

P.P.S. Also, can you ask Jesus why Julie is so sick?
She's been in bed for two days because she has to
puke every time she gets out of bed. I know it
will pass. Then it will happen all over again. And
it isn't fair. She hasn't done anything to deserve it.
Tell Jesus that. Nicely.

Cassie Callahan
Hamilton, MO
July 28

Dear Son of a Grump,

Don't blame my mom! I still think your dad is the one
who broke off their engagement. Otherwise, Mom
wouldn't have left like she did and cried all the time
like she did and still is. I will make you a deal. I will write
to my mom for details, but only if you do the same
with your dad. And you can just ask him straight-out
because at least he's there with you.

I've been thinking about the first time I met you and
Julie. Everybody in our school was pretty curious about
the new teacher in town and the new teacher's kids.
Most of our teachers were so old that they'd had our
parents in class 100 years ago. You should have heard all
the rumors going around town about you guys. It didn't
hurt that your dad was a single parent, divorced but
raising the kids. You can imagine all the stories they
made up about a mom who would leave her kids and
remarry a rich guy who worked in a foreign location
like Paris, France. Actually, we thought that sounded
exotic (my word from last Tuesday, BTW).

We all wanted to have your dad for a teacher, even
though nobody had ever met him. Was he surprised that
he was the only male teacher in Hamilton Elementary?
Should have known he'd teach sixth grade. I didn't

realize that you'd be in my grade until you strolled into
our classroom, and I didn't even know Julie was your
sister until the next week, when your dad picked you
guys up.

I thought you were stuck up and full of yourself
that first day because you didn't talk to any of us.
You acted like you were already fed up with living in a
small town, and you'd only just gotten here. That's why
I was the first one to toss out an insult—couldn't help
myself. Although, looking back now, if I had it to do
over again . . . (Remind me later to tell you what Pastor
Mike said about wholesome speech.) We had picture day,
and when you looked at yours, you said, "Could you take
another one, please? This one doesn't do me justice."

I was next in line, and I said, "You don't need justice.
You need mercy."

Half a dozen kids behind me heard what I said,
and none of them got it. But you did. You knew the
difference between justice and mercy. You turned to
face me, and for the first time, you laughed. Hard. The
guy took your picture that exact second, and I think it
showed every one of your teeth.

It didn't take you long to retaliate (Monday's word,
which means "get even" or "strike back"). You stuck
around and looked at the picture of me the photo guy
was showing me on his camera. Then, totally serious, you
said, "Hmmm. Your face."

"What?" I demanded. "What's wrong with my face?"
I thought it was a pretty good picture.

"There's only one thing wrong with it," you said, making me wait. "It shows."

I stuck out my hand, and we shook. "I'm Cassie," I said.

"Nick. And I know who you are," you said. "I never forget a face." You started walking away, then called back, "But in your case, I'll make an exception."

Do you remember all that? We should have declared ourselves "steps" right then. Forget our mixed-up parents.

I'll stop writing now. I'm going to work on a letter to Mom, and you'd better do the same with your dad.

Still,
Cassie

P.S. But first I need to write Julie.

Cassie Callahan
Hamilton, MO
July 28

Dear Julie,

I think you should get Nick to read this to you instead
of your dad. Nick says your dad has turned into a
grump. I hope he's not being grumpy with you.

Kirby still misses you so much. She sleeps with the
squeaky mouse you gave her. Mom said she read in her
dog book that black lab puppies are supposed to stop
growing after six months, but I don't think Kirby read
that book. She is gigantic and getting bigger every
day. Think Clifford on steroids. Or maybe vitamins
(because I'm not sure what steroids are—Nick heard
about them on the sports channel). I can tell Kirby
really misses you because whenever I let her out in the
backyard, she runs straight to your swing and sniffs and
whines and sometimes lies down right under your swing,
where you should be.

And that makes me sadder than sad because I know
how she feels.

Do you remember the first time you and I met?
I'd stayed late after school, but I can't remember why.
I think I'd called Jeremy Carlson a meathead, but he
really is one because he was a bully then and is still
a bully now. Anyway, when I finally got to go home,
I walked out the front of the school, and there you

were, standing in the grass and leaning against the building like you were holding up the brick wall. The sun was shining, and a ray lit you up like a spotlight, and for a minute, I thought you were an angel, with that wispy blonde hair and delicate everything.

Then somebody ran up past me, right toward you, like he was going to crash into you. Your eyes got so big. I was afraid you'd break into a million pieces. So I ran after the kid and pushed him down just before he reached you. That's when I saw it was Nick. I had already met him in class and in the picture-taking line. Only I didn't know that he was your brother yet. So I shouted at him, "Leave her alone! What's wrong with you?"

He got up, brushed himself off. "What's wrong with YOU?"

"You can't just run into people! Especially little people who could get really hurt!" I moved between you two, like I was your protector.

"What's it to you? If I want to beat her up, I'll beat her up." But Nick couldn't keep from smiling a little.

"It's okay," you said. "But thanks. I'm Julie."

I turned to you then. "I'm Cassie. And it's not okay to be bullied."

Nick darted in front of me, grabbed you up, and spun you around. "And I'm Nick the Powerful!"

I think I would have tackled him again if your dad hadn't come out of the school right then and shouted, "Come on, guys! Time to go home!"

Nick took your hand and said, "Let's go, Shorty."

65

"She's not short! She's young!" I called after you, because even then I maybe knew it's not just punches and shoves that bully people. Words can bully people too.

Don't let those private-school kids call you Shorty or anything else. Or I'll come up there and they'll be sorry!

Kirby and I miss you like crazy, Julie.

Love ya,
Cassie

P.S. I put that "ya" there because I felt embarrassed just writing "love." But I do, you know.

Cassie Callahan
Hamilton, MO, where she lives with her aged
grandmother
July 28

Dear King of Insults,

I can't believe you're doing your season finale in
Hannibal, Missouri! I live in Hamilton, Missouri, which people
get mixed up with Hannibal all the time! Hannibal is about
two and a half hours from my house, three and a half
if Gram's driving. Mom and I have driven through there
lots of times because it's on the way to Illinois, where
Grandma and Grandpa Callahan live. Mom used to tell
me we were taking a little vacation, but it would end up
being a trick and we'd just drive to Grandma Callahan's
in Peoria, Illinois.

But I've been to Hannibal for real, too. Mom took
me to see Mark Twain's house, where they've got his
typewriter and everything. I love Mark Twain! We will
watch your show this week and find out more details.
I think your producer is pretty clever to send you to
the crazy-named towns all over. And he (or she) is a
genius sending you to Hannibal.

I thought I'd miss Julie and Nick less the more
time they're gone. I was wrong. Have you ever missed
anybody? I mean, I know you're the Insult King, but did
you ever have somebody you didn't feel like insulting?

The day after Travis left and took my two best
friends with him, I was so mad that I took my framed

photo of Travis and threw it on the floor. It shattered in a million pieces. I picked up the big pieces of glass, but there were all these tiny pieces left. So I took a slice of bread and pressed it to the floor, and all the tiny pieces stuck to the bread. This was not my idea. Mom wrote it in her household tricks column, Just Jen around the House.

Anyway, I think having an insult contest is a fabonomous idea. Bet it wasn't yours.

Ha!
Cassie

P.S. Remember how Nick said you promised you'd send me a birthday present? Well, my birthday is August 31, and yours will probably be the only present I get, because I won't have a birthday party and my mom won't even be here.

P.P.S. Here's what God said about promises to give someone a present: "A person who promises a gift but doesn't give it is like clouds and wind that bring no rain" (Proverbs 25:14).

P.P.P.S. I have a sneaking suspicion that Gram has been reading the letters you sent me. I think that's against the law. But she is bigger than me.

Emma Hendren
Hamilton, MO
July 29

Dear Johnathan,

You ask a lot of questions for an insult king.

You think you're old? I'm so old I remember when
rainbows only came in black and white.

I grew up in Hamilton and married my high school
sweetheart and settled in the house I was born in. After my
husband died, I worked in the Hamilton Café until I bought
it from the owners, who wanted to retire. Ran that place
for 20 years and made a success of it. Now I volunteer at
the community health center run by our church. And I do
crossword puzzles. And raise an almost 11-year-old girl, who
gives me a run for my money.

One of your questions was about Cassie not going to
parties. The girl refuses to go to her friends' birthday parties
because she insists she doesn't want one of her own. I think
it's because her mother won't be back by August 31. I've
offered to let Cassie have whatever kind of party she wants,
even a sleepover, which for me would be a supreme sacrifice.
But she says no way. I asked Jen to come home, but her boss
took advantage of Jen's being in California and committed
her to speaking at some big newspaper convention out there.
(Jen has a syndicated column about using weird things

to clean the house and solve household problems. It's called Just Jen around the House. I wish she'd use a can of cola or a lemon peel to fix _my_ household problem, which is raising her daughter.)

As to why Travis lit out of here like a house afire, your guess is as good as mine. And mine isn't very good. Those two were made for each other, so I thought. It took Jen a long, long time to get over the loss of her first husband. It better not take that long to get over this one.

You also asked (come to think of it, you really do ask a heap of questions—you're not an undercover census taker, are you?) about Julie, Nick's little sister. I find it interesting that Cassie would write you about her. Julie is the sweetest little thing you'd ever want to meet. She was born with a kidney disease and a neurological syndrome that left her nearly deaf at age three. She's got good hearing aids now but still doesn't hear everything. I used to say that gal gave me a second chance to be a better person. I'd say something insulting or harsh, without thinking about it. Julie wouldn't hear me, so she'd smile that sweet smile of hers and say, "What did you say, Gram?" She called me Gram even before Travis and Jen got engaged. Then I'd get a second chance to be a better person, and I'd say, "I love you, sugar." And she'd say back, "I love you, Gram."

Drat that Travis and Jen!

Have a nice day.

Emma

Cassie Callahan
Stuck in Hamilton, MO
July 29

Dear Mom,

Have you found yourself yet?

Gram just gave me a hard time telling me not to give you a hard time. She said I shouldn't write anything sad or whiny. So I guess this letter will be very short.

I miss Julie.

I miss Nick.

I even miss Travis.

Okay. I miss you, too.

Don't forget that Kirby is only a puppy, kind of. She did something on the rug in your bedroom, and you wouldn't like hearing about it so I won't tell you. But she is very sorry.

I need you to tell me something for honest and true. Why did Travis dump you? Was it me? Nick thinks you dumped Travis, but if you did, what did he do to make him so dumpable? Please send me your answer in writing. I'm still not in the mood to talk on the phone.

Love ya,
Cassie

Nick Barton
Chicago Old Folks' Home
August 1

'Sup, Callahan,

Guess what! Your mom's weird household remedy
column is in the Chicago newspaper! Did you know
that? Maybe she really is famous. Why aren't
you rich?

I'm the one who saw the article in the paper
yesterday while I was looking for the comics. She
wrote about a bunch of things you can do to clean
stuff with a can of cola.

I read it out loud to Grandad and Julie. Julie
said it was fabonomous, and Grandad went to see if
he had any cola so he could finally get the oil off
his driveway where his car leaked it. When Dad
got home, I tried to give him the article, but he
said he didn't want to read it. But this morning I
found yesterday's newspaper folded to that page
with the Just Jen around the House column, and I
didn't do it.

I'm enclosing the article in case you want it.

I did what you wanted me to: I asked Dad
why your mom dumped us. But I think my timing
was off—I asked him right after he didn't read
your mom's article. He just mumbled something
that could have been "Not now, Nick." Or maybe,

"New cow's sick." He's getting harder and harder to understand. I plan to leave him a note in his lunch box, asking him in writing and telling him to answer in writing too.

Julie says hey—
Nick

JUST JEN AROUND THE HOUSE

I know a lot of people are down on colas of all kinds, but I'll bet most of you still have the stuff around your house. Good! Because here are a few uses you may not have known about for that can or bottle of cola:

Did your car leak oil onto your driveway? Yeah, you could buy sand and let it sit there, then scrub it off. *Or*, pull out your can or big bottle of cola. Pour it onto the oil and let it sit for a couple of hours. Then rinse. Good as new! (Now park somewhere else, or go get the car fixed.)

Who loves scrubbing toilets? Okay, hands down. You don't need to buy those expensive cleaners. Just pour a can of cola into the toilet. Let it sit a spell. (Don't use it—you can hold it.) Brush, then flush. Voilà—troubles down the drain!

Need a new faucet? That old one looking grungy and moldy? Wait a minute! You guessed it. Bring out the cola and pour it on. Watch the yucky stuff bubble, fizz, and go away.

Car battery corroded? Think you need a new one? Those things are expensive, you know! Instead, pour your favorite cola and wait for the stuff to do the trick. You're off and running!

Drink it?

73

Cassie Callahan
Hamilton, MO
August 3

Hey, Nick!

Thanks for asking your dad about breaking the
engagement. Any word from him yet? I'm still waiting
on an answer from Mom.

It's good that you guys saw Mom's column in the
Chicago Tribune. Thanks for sending that. I was worried
she'd lose her job and we'd get dumped from our home
and everything. And I've been dumped enough for one
summer, thank you very much.

I sent a follow-up letter to Jesus asking him about
Julie and why she has to be so sick all the time. I was
pretty straight with him and told him that we didn't
think it was very fair to have Julie be the sick one
because she's nicer than you and me put together.
I said I knew Julie had never done anything wrong,
especially since she hadn't even been born when she
got the bad genes. So I asked him whose fault it was
anyway, and even though I was thinking maybe your
mom's or even your dad's, I didn't suggest it.

After youth group, Pastor Mike read my letter to
Jesus and didn't make me change a word, even though
he's always talking about choosing words wisely, and I
admit I didn't really think much about that when I was
writing Jesus.

When Pastor Mike finished reading my letter, he gave me a hint and said to look up John 9. I went right home and read that whole chapter, and I think I get it. It's about this guy who'd been blind since birth. Then he meets Jesus, and Jesus heals him right up. And the guy can see, and he's so excited. But the important part is where the disciples ask Jesus why the man is blind. They even ask if it's the guy's fault or his parents' fault, like it must be one or the other. Only Jesus surprises them and says, "Neither!" It's not anybody's fault. He's blind so the power of God can be seen in him. And Jesus ends up healing him, but nobody except the ex-blind guy is excited about it. They say, "That's not the same guy!" And even his parents say, "Don't ask us about who healed our son. Ask him." And when the ex-blind guy says, "Well, I'm telling you, Jesus made me see!" they kick him out of church.

I admit I'm shaky on the next part, but Jesus told the bigwigs in the church that they were the ones who couldn't see, and that they would be sorry. And man, were they insulted!

Anyway, the best part I understood was that being sick isn't anybody's fault. And there might even be some secret meaning to the whole thing. I still might write Pastor Mike about it. But I always had the idea that if I were Julie's stepsister and we shared a room, I might end up becoming a better person, more like Julie.

Only now we'll never know about that.

I would have put my money on it being your mom's fault, if you want to know the truth. But I guess not.

Speaking of your mom, which we don't do much, or ever, do you ever hear from her? Gram says she saw your mom in a potato chip commercial on TV, and she sure was skinny. Gram said, "I guarantee she didn't sneak and eat a single potato chip during the break. She's so skinny she could slide through a knothole if she wasn't wearing shoes." Ha ha.

Cassie

P.S. Here's what I found out about <u>The Last Insult Standing</u>. It's going to be a live show where wannabe insult comics compete. Won't that be cool? I'll bet we could win. Ha ha! Plus, it's going to be in Hannibal, Missouri, on account of that being where Mark Twain lived and he had good insults and one-liners. "I have been through some terrible things in my life, some of which actually happened."

P.P.S. You should write Kirby the Insult King about it, because I'm running out of insults for him.

So I did like John 9, only it's confusing, too, the more I think about it. How can being sick not be anybody's fault? Where does sick come from, then? And I'm not crazy about the second song we sang this morning. Do we really need all six verses? Gram put a pot roast in the oven before church, and it will be done at noon, so she won't like it if you go overtime. Just sayin'.

Dear Cassie,

I got your message in the offering plate, although I couldn't quite make out all of it. I did, however, get the gist. I'm glad you liked John 9.

In case you haven't noticed, earth is not perfect, like heaven is. You've heard of the Fall, when sin entered the world, haven't you? God created a perfect world, but he gave people free will, so they wouldn't be robots. People messed up, and so our world is messed up, and disease and decay became part of the natural order of things.

I know. That probably wasn't the answer you were looking for, but don't forget—I'm just a mouthpiece. I still have trouble accepting illness and death too.

Pastor Mike

P.S. Did the pot roast burn?

Kirby the Dog
Hamilton, MO
August 4

Dear Kirby the Insult King,

Cassie and I watched your show last night, <u>The Hour of Insult</u>, filmed in Why, Arizona. Three times we heard you use "dog" in a pejorative fashion. (PEJORATIVE means "not nice," and it was Cassie's word of the day today, as it happens.) We did not appreciate the canine jokes. And we did not find them at all amusing.

Kirby

P.S. Dog hair on your couch is no reason to get rid of your pet! Put on rubber gloves and pet the couch. All the hairs will come right up. (This tip has been brought to you by Jennifer Callahan's column, Just Jen around the House.)

P.P.S. Mark Twain said, "If you pick up a starving dog and make him prosperous, he will not bite you. This is the principal difference between a dog and a man."

Nick Barton
Chicago, IL
August 3

Callahan!

Did you watch tonight's episode of The Hour of
Insult? Dad was home, so I had to go to the old
folks' rec room and watch with the old people. But
they're pretty cool. They laughed in all the right
places. And—get this!—Grandad loves the show!
He watched it with me and laughed harder than
anybody! Who would have thought, right?

I sure hope you were watching when they told
about filming the contest The Last Insult Standing
in Hannibal! I think you and I really could win that
contest! We have to at least try. They're going
to pick five guys and five "ladies" to compete. To
enter the competition, you have to send them 10
insults. That's it! The contest people will pick the
contestants on the basis of those insults. Then guys
face off against guys, and girls against girls. Let's
do it! I know what you're thinking. Your mom and
my dad hate insults, so they won't help us. Well,
we'll just have to help ourselves. They've pretty
much left us on our own anyway.

On a less exciting note, when I got up this
morning and came down for breakfast, there
was a letter waiting for me on the counter, a

letter from Dad, even though he was still upstairs sleeping. I am enclosing his letter. Some of it may make you madder at him. But don't forget that you're the one who asked me to ask him, so you can't get mad at me.

Sorry,
Nick

P.S. Say hi to your gram for me. I kind of miss her.

P.P.S. Don't forget to play fetch with Kirby. I'm the one who taught her to chase Frisbees.

To: My son, Nick
From: Your dad

Nick,

I'm sorry that I couldn't talk about this face-to-face. Maybe someday. I hope soon. Right now I'm having trouble talking to anyone about anything. And I'm sorry about that. You don't deserve the way I've been acting. I know I've been taking things out on you, which is why I've tried to say as little as possible.

Things are hard on all of us, even your grandad, who's been kind enough to give us a place to live and to give me a job. But I miss teaching. I know I've been on edge, and that can't be easy on you and Julie. I will try to do better.

You asked me why Jen and I broke our engagement, and I'm not sure how satisfying my answer will be. The short answer is that Jen told me that she didn't want to go through with our wedding. To be honest, it came as a shock. I thought she and I understood each other and wanted the same things out of life. I know she loved you and Julie. I certainly loved her and Cassie.

You're too young to remember much about when your mother and I were married, and I suppose that's a good thing. It wasn't very pleasant around our house. But your mom and I did love each other, and it shook my world when she left me. It hurt you and Julie, too. That's why I didn't date for a long time. I didn't want any of us to go through that again.

Then I met Jen. We were instant friends. The first time I saw her was when I took you to Cassie's birthday party. She'd invited your whole class, and I made you go. I was walking toward the house with you when we heard the party going in the backyard. So we went around back, and there was this woman in a clown suit, with a frizzy red wig and enough face paint to coat a house. She came over, handed you a balloon, and said, "Don't just stand there! Blow!" Then she handed me a fistful of unblown balloons. I ended up staying and learning how to make balloon giraffes. I didn't even know she was Cassie's mother until she brought out the cake and Cassie said, "Thanks, Mom." I thought she was a hired clown.

I admit I was pleasantly surprised the next time I saw her, which was at teacher conference night. Jen's a head-turner. I asked another teacher who she was and laughed out loud when I realized she was the clown.

Not sure why I told you all that.

Except to help you understand why I had to leave, why _we_ had to leave. It took me years to get over being dumped by your mother, Nick. I couldn't go through that again.

The night before I packed you guys into the car and drove to Chicago, Jen told me she had to talk to me. I thought I'd done something wrong. Or maybe she'd decided she didn't want us to live in her house, that she wanted us to buy a new house or something. We went for a walk, and it took her over a mile to come out with it. Finally, she burst into tears and said she didn't know if she could go through with it. "Through with what?" I asked. "Our wedding," she said.

And that was it. I turned on my heels and walked home. I stayed up all night packing. In the morning, I told you we were moving to Chicago.

Now you know why. When I met Jen, I believed I'd finally found someone I could be with forever. I thought she felt the same way, but it turned out that wasn't the case. After Jen broke up with me, I thought it would be too hard for you and Julie to keep going to school with Cassie and seeing Jen, constantly being reminded of the family you almost had. And to be honest, it would have been too hard for me, too. So that's why we're in Chicago.

Love,
Dad

Jen Callahan
San Bernardino, CA
August 2

Dearest Cassie,

Honey, you must never think that breaking the engagement was your fault! Are you kidding? Travis thought so highly of you that sometimes I wondered if you were the reason he wanted to marry me!

I'm so sorry you're unhappy. But I really think that being with Gram is the best thing for you right now. I need some time to sort myself out and figure out what our life is going to be like now that our plans have changed. Your grandmother can be feisty and even caustic (if you haven't come across "caustic" in your Word-a-Day calendar yet, look it up). But she's good people, and I trust her to take good care of you during this difficult time.

Cassie, you asked me why Travis broke our engagement, and although I don't really understand it completely myself, I'll tell you what I do know. That last day, our last day together, I couldn't stop thinking about your father. Greg and I were so young when we fell in love and got married. We had our whole lives ahead of us. The plans we shared, and the dreams we made! Greg wanted to invent things—he was really smart, honey. He had plans drawn up for everything from a better mousetrap to a way to find your keys when they're missing. (I think someone else has invented that now.) I knew he would be another Thomas Edison one day.

We were as poor as church mice when we found out I was pregnant with you. And all we felt was pure joy. At the time, we were renting a tiny trailer house in Rosewood Gardens, and I was going to school at the community college and working full time. That's when Gram took us in, and it's a good thing she did. I'll tell you about those days sometime. When you were born, it was the best day of our lives. Your father loved you like crazy. Even when his inventions kept getting turned down, he didn't let it get him down. He was a good man.

But then your dad took that night job in Chillicothe so I could stay in school. It was when he was coming back at night on Old 36 that the truck rammed into him. The accident changed everything, changed me especially.

Since then, I've devoted my life to you and to my writing career. I've kept your dad's last name, Callahan, and I'd never dated another man until I met Travis. I'd never wanted to. At first, going places and being with Travis didn't even feel like dating. It just felt good. I fell in love with him before I knew what hit me.

I think you wanted me to marry Travis just as much as I wanted to marry him. I thought we'd all live happily ever after.

But back to that night. All day, thoughts of your father filled my mind and my heart. Here I was about to marry another man. What if I was making a huge mistake?

I had to talk to Travis about it. I wanted to be honest with him and tell him what I was feeling. I knew I wasn't betraying Greg—of course I wasn't. But that's how I felt. And I'd always been able to tell Travis how I felt.

Only he didn't want to hear me. I tried to explain. More than anything, I wanted him to understand. I needed him to talk to me. Instead, without a word, he turned his back on me and walked away. The next day, when I called him to meet and talk things out, he didn't answer his cell. Then Gram told me that he'd taken Julie and Nick and moved to Chicago. I thought she was joking—I really did. I haven't heard from Travis since that night.

So there you have it.

I love you more than anything, honey.

Love,
Mom

P.S. Keep that dog out of my bedroom!

Johnathan Kirby, King of Insults
Bagdad, AZ
July 31

Kid Callahan,

Stop with the hints about your birthday, will ya?

So your big day is August 31, huh? That just happens to be the day we're filming <u>The Last Insult Standing</u> in Hannibal. So, I'm sending you two tickets to the show. Good seats too. You can invite a friend, if you have any. So now you can lay off the gift idea. You're welcome.

Since you asked, I will tell you that I have had two people in my life who never deserved an insult. One was my mother. If there's anyone in heaven with your Pen Pal, it will be Ma. She never wrote God or Jesus that I know about, but she read everything <u>they</u> wrote. She didn't approve of my insults, but she was enough of a regular Joe to laugh when they were funny.

The other insult-free zone was around my little sister. <u>But I don't feel like writing about her.</u> Anyways, I wasted enough ink writing this.

The King

P.S. Sorry I didn't wrap the tickets. Where am I supposed to find wrapping paper in Bagdad?

Johnathan Kirby
Continental Divide, NM
August 1

Dear Emma,

Out of all the letters I get, yours are the only ones I never swear at when I get them. I'm starting not to swear at Cassie's, either. Or Nick's. Maybe.

I sure am getting tired of traveling to these weird towns, let me tell you. You may have been wondering why my letters come from towns with such crazy names. You would have to ask Marty the Smarty, my producer, to get the answer to that one. He's not speaking to me at the moment. He just told me his big plan for filming next year's <u>Hour of Insult,</u> and I just told him that if I decided to kill myself, I'd climb his ego and jump to his IQ.

Here are some of the towns he's booking me in next year:

Mosquitoville, Vermont
Fleatown, Ohio
Flea Valley, California
Ticktown, Virginia
Tick Bite, North Carolina
Bug Hill, North Carolina
Roach, Nevada
Roaches, Illinois

Cricket Corner, New Hampshire
Cricket Hill, Virginia
Grasshopper Junction, Arizona
Shoofly, North Carolina
Spider, Kentucky
Spiderweb, South Carolina

I was surprised to learn that the kid's, Cassie's,
birthday is the same day as my big show, <u>The Last</u>
<u>Insult Standing</u>. Upon discovering this, I sent
Cassie two tickets to the show. I don't know how
far Hamilton really is from Hannibal, I'll admit.
But how far can it be? They're both in Missouri.
Maybe you could drive her. I don't have many—any—
friends, and I kind of like writing you like you are
one. Just pen pals, of course. Never too old to have
a pal.

You know what Sam Clemens, aka Mark Twain, said
about that, don't you? "Age is a matter of mind over
matter. If you don't mind, it don't matter."

So, how 'bout it, Emma? Will I see you in
Hannibal?

Your friend,
Johnny

Cassie Callahan
Hamilton, MO
August 5

Nick!

Let's do it! Let's enter that contest!

Did you hear that the winner of <u>The Last Insult Standing</u> gets a 10-day cruise for the entire family? Think about it, Nick! We could get both of our parents on that cruise! We could convince the producers that we're all family! I know we could. I know if I won, Mom would love to have you and Julie come on the cruise with us, and then Travis would have to come along too. (Same thing if you won, of course.) Either way, we'd have 10 days together! AND, maybe after spending 10 days together, Travis and Mom would remember what it used to be like. And who knows?

I know. I'm getting way ahead of myself.

By now, you must have gotten the letter from Mom I sent on to you. I read your dad's side. I'm not sure what to think. Only, I think they're both being stupidheads. Don't you? It's like they each think the other person doesn't want them around. I wish we could do something about it. Any ideas on that front?

In the meantime, let's work on our lists of 10 best insults. The deadline is right around the corner!

Insultingly yours,
Cassie

P.S. NEWS FLASH! I just got the mail, and you'll never guess what King Kirby sent me—tickets to <u>The Last Insult Standing</u>! Two tickets! I guess if you and I make it as finalists, we won't need the tickets, but it was nice of him to send them. I think if I play my poor-me-with-no-mom-and-no-birthday-party card, I can get Gram to drive me to Hannibal. But what about you? How are you going to get from Chicago to Hannibal?

Julie Barton
Retirement Community
Chicago, IL
August 4

Dear Cassie,

Thank you so much for that great get-well
card you and Gram sent! I laughed so hard I got
a coughing fit. (But it was worth it.) I haven't
hurled in two days, and I'm eating applesauce and
yogurt, too.

Will you guys please send me a picture of
Kirby? With you standing next to her? That way
I can see how much she's grown. I wish I would
grow that much.

I love that you're writing to Jesus. I wish I
could read better so I could read his letters in
the Bible too.

In case you're wondering, Nick is writing this.
He told me about you guys wanting to go to
Hannibal to see that TV show. Wouldn't it be great
if you could meet up there? I was hoping I could
go too. I'd love to see you and Gram! But I talked
Nick into asking Dad if he'd take us to Hannibal
to see the show, and that was a big mistake. Dad
doesn't like that show. Still, I think he might have
said okay until he put two and two together and
figured out he'd probably run into you guys there.

Not that he doesn't like all of you. (Nick here. Julie said "love" instead of "like," but I couldn't make myself write it. Right now, it doesn't feel like Dad loves OR likes anybody or anything, not even me and Julie.) I think Dad misses you as much as I do. And that's a whole lot.

I need to go now. (Nick here: Julie just got walloped with one of her king-size headaches, so the place she needs to go now is to bed. Hold on, she's giving me a P.S.)

Love,
Julie

P.S. I told Dad I liked the uniforms of the new school he's putting us in. But I really don't.

Nick Barton
Old Folks' Home
Chicago, IL
August 7

Dear Cassie,

I've been working on my list of 10 insults, and this is it. So if you think I should scratch any of these and come up with a new one, you'll have to call or write me real quick because we're running out of time. You should get yours in right away too. I'm pretty sure that some of these insults may be things you've said to me, but I'm not sure, and I don't know which ones came from you in the first place. So call me if I've written an insult that's yours. I'll take it off my list. Promise. That's why I put in extras.

Here goes:

I'll bet it takes you an hour to cook Minute Rice.

Take a long walk off a short pier.

The last time I saw a face like yours, I fed it a banana.

If you were any dumber, you'd have to be twins.

Are you going to sue the guy? (What guy?) The guy who ran over your face.

When they were handing out looks, you thought they said "books," and you asked for a funny one. OR: When they were handing out noses, you thought they said "roses," so you asked for a big, smelly one.

You are really down to earth . . . just not far enough.

You're so clueless that you got fired from the M&M'S factory for throwing away all the W's.

You're so ugly that when you were born, the doctor slapped your mother (who, BTW, had sold her car for gas money).

You're so ugly, I'll bet when your mom dropped you off at school, she got a fine for littering.

Julie told you about Dad refusing to drive us to Hannibal to see the show. (He'd go nuts if he knew I might be IN the show.) What Julie didn't say was that Dad exploded. "Hannibal is in Missouri!" he shouted. "HAMILTON is in Missouri! What if Cassie talks Jen into taking her there to see the Insult King? Did you think about that? I can't see Jen now. I won't do it! I can't go through this all over again!"

"But Cassie's mother is in California," I explained logically and calmly. "She won't even be in Missouri."

"You can't know that, Nick!" Dad screamed. "I will never go back to Missouri! Not ever! Never!

You got that?" Then he stormed out of the old folks' home and didn't come back for hours. Poor Julie was afraid he'd never come back.

So I've moved to Plan B. I have some money saved up from mowing lawns. Plus birthday money from Grandad. I think it will be enough for a bus ticket to Hannibal.

See you there!

Nick

P.S. Be honest about the insults and let me know if something doesn't work! We both have to win this thing!

Cassie Callahan
Hamilton, MO
August 10

King Nick,

You nailed it! I think Johnathan Kirby better watch out! His throne is in jeopardy (my word for the day). I hope you mailed in your insults, including the last two, which were some of the best, if you ask me. Way to go, Nick!

You're coming alone, by bus? You are fearless! You don't know the meaning of the word FEAR. (On the other hand, you don't know the meaning of a lot of words. Ha ha!)

You've probably figured out that the money in this envelope is to make sure you can afford a bus ticket from Chicago to Hannibal. Or maybe there's a train, and now you can afford a ticket for that! Gram has been paying me for doing chores that Mom makes me do for free. I spent some on a roll of postage stamps, but I don't need the rest of it, so don't worry about paying me back. It will be payment enough seeing you onstage in Hannibal.

I'd like to be there too, but I don't know if I will. I didn't exactly do what they said to do to enter the contest. I don't know. I wrote up a list of insults, but when I read over it, it didn't sound funny to me. It sounded . . . kind of mean. Definitely not wholesome. Something a bully might say to Julie. That's all I could think about. This thinking about words thing is tough. Insults have always been easy.

I flipped through the Bible, looking for great insults like "whitewashed tomb" and "sons of vipers." Nothing. So after youth group, I asked Pastor Mike, and he showed me how there's this kind of dictionary in the back of those Bibles they gave us for joining up. He said it was a concordance. You look up a word, like PRAYER, and it gives you all the verses that have PRAYER in them—and there's a lot, let me tell you.

At home, I looked up INSULTS but got nothing. Then I tried DUMB, LOSER, and other words like those, but that didn't work either. So I tried SPEECH and WORDS, and man, did that work, but not like I'd hoped. Here are some of the things I found:

Let your conversation be gracious and attractive so that you will have the right response for everyone.
Colossians 4:6

Let everything you say be good and helpful, so that your words will be an encouragement to those who hear them.
Ephesians 4:29

See what I mean? But this one is cool:

Whoever loves a pure heart and gracious speech will have the king as a friend.
Proverbs 22:11

98

Think I should send it to the King of Insults?

Still, I did my best. I have my ticket for the show. So I will be there in Hannibal—if not onstage, in the audience cheering for you!

Your fan,
Cassie

P.S. Now we need to talk about Travis and Mom. After reading both their letters, I am more convinced than ever that if there's a chance of getting them back together, it's up to us! Mom and Travis should be writing (or calling or texting) each other and saying what they said in their letters to us. But they're both too stubborn. Or too hurt. Or too messed up in their grown-up ways. And so . . . what if you and I write for them? Ta da!

Cassie Callahan
Hamilton, MO
August 10

Dear Producer of <u>The Last Insult Standing</u>,

I'll bet you guys have brains that are as good as new
. . . because you sure haven't used them to think
through this insult contest. Insulting is an art. The best
insults are person-specific, not generic or appearing
in a list of 10. I know. You'll tell me you worked hard
coming up with your plan. I say you did the work of
three men: Larry, Moe, and Curly (the Three Stooges,
in case you don't get out much).

   Also, although Hannibal, hometown of Mark Twain
(who said, "I didn't attend the funeral, but I sent a nice
letter saying I approved of it") is the perfect place
for the show, you neglected to give the address of
the studio, or wherever you plan to film this thing. So,
what, is it like at the corner of Walk and Don't Walk?
Inquiring contestants want to know.

   Look, here's what's wrong with making us list 10
insults and then you choosing the best list. Suppose
I list an insult like this: "What happened, buddy? Did
you suntan through the kitchen screen?" But the
other contestant doesn't have freckles. Did you think
of that?

   Or if I tell someone, "I'll bet your eyeballs have
blonde roots, Blondie." But she's not blonde. Or dumb.
   Not funny.

On the other hand, take a line like "The lights are on, but nobody's home." Not a big chuckle on the page, right? But delivered at exactly the right time to exactly the right person, and your audience would crack up.

Since my best friend's list of 10 insults contained five that appeared on my initial list, I decided to let him go ahead and use the insults to enter your stupidhead contest, and you had better pick him as a finalist. (His name is Nick Barton. Don't forget it.) If not, I will be writing your mother and quoting Mae West, who said, "You should have thrown him away and kept the stork."

Disappointed,
Cassie Callahan

P.S. Don't thank me for insulting you. It's been my pleasure.

P.P.S. I think there are 10 insults in this letter if you quit goofing off long enough to count them. And don't forget to count this one.

Cassie Callahan
Hamilton, MO
August 10

Dear Julie,

I wrote this letter three times, but tore it up because
I didn't want to say the wrong thing. (And Nick, if
you're reading this to Julie like you should, here's
another great reason to write letters. You can tear
them up if you say the wrong thing. Can't tear up
phone conversations, can you?)

I've been thinking a lot about insults lately. They've
always come easy to me—too easy, Mom says. Like the
words are out of my mouth before my brain gets in on
it. I've never meant to be mean with the insults—just
funny. But lately, I've been wondering if something I
say that I think is hilarious lands on the other person
as mean.

So I decided to ask you. I've seen you get slammed,
teased, and insulted at school. And although Nick and I
are quick to attack anybody who says anything mean
to you, you always take it with a smile, like it doesn't
matter.

But does it? On the inside? Even when you laugh
along, are you laughing inside, Julie?

I never wondered this before, but I do now. I need to
know how insults make you feel.

And if I've ever hurt your feelings by saying something I thought was funny, I will cut out my tongue. Or maybe I'll just cut out Nick's.

Love ya,
Cassie

Julie in Chicago
(And Nick)
August 13

Dear Cassie,

I am glad you sent me that letter about insults, although it makes me miss you even more.

First, I want you to know that you have never hurt my feelings with one of your insults. You couldn't, because I know you love me. (Nick here: Julie admits that I've hurt her feelings a few times, even though she knows I love her. I feel pretty rotten about that and never even suspected it. I sure won't call her Shorty or any other name again, except Julie. And if I do, I'll cut my own tongue out.)

Julie again—Cassie, I know you would never want to hurt me. Even if Dad and your mom never speak to each other again, you will always be my sister.

You ask how I can smile when kids make fun of me or tease me about the way I talk, or the way I learn, or how I have to leave the class for different therapies. Your mom told me once that when bullies say mean things to me, a simple smile can let the air out of their balloons. She said they want to get me all mad and upset, and they're disappointed when they see me smile. Besides, some "insults" are funny. Some are not.

You've made me think about this—why some insults or name-callings bounce off and make me smile, and why other insults make me sad. Here's one answer I came up with—the meanest insults are the ones that are a little bit true.

Once when I ate more pizza than you and Nick did, you called me "Pizza Piggy." I still grin when I think of that night with you and Nick and your mom and Dad. And me—the Pizza Piggy. If I weren't so skinny, maybe my feelings would have been hurt. But since I'm so not fat—no piece of truth in that insult—it was funny.

On the other hand, I still remember the day in kindergarten when it hit me that I didn't talk like the other kids. Dad and Nick had always been so nice to me. They'd never said a word about me being hard to understand. I don't think I realized I left off letters at the ends of words ("wan" for want; "hoe" for home). So I raised my hand to answer the teacher's question. Not even she understood my answer. Michael, the redheaded boy in front of me, turned in his seat and called me "Mush Mouth." It was an insult that hurt my feelings all year.

Nick here: Julie left to go lie down. She said to tell you she loves you and not to worry about her.

Why is everything so mixed up?

Nick

Nick Barton
Chicago, IL
August 13

Dear Cassie,

Today I got your letter with your idea about us
writing our parents and pretending to be them.
At first, I thought you'd gone off the edge of
crazy. But the more I think about it, the more
I think you just might be onto something. They
both need to know what the other one is thinking,
and they're too mixed up to figure it out on
their own.
    What have we got to lose, right?
    I think you better write my dad, though. He'd
know right away that I was the one writing him,
if I did it. Besides, I'd have to mail the letter from
here, so it would be postmarked Chicago. I will
do my best writing your mother. If you tried to
write her, pretending to be Dad, she'd know right
away it was you because of the big words. So
I'm Travis, writing your mom. You're Jen, writing
my dad. And at least the Chicago postmark will
be right. Do it! Soon we should hear back from
The Last Insult Standing.

                          Signed,
                          Nick, aka Travis

Emma Hendren
Hamilton, MO
August 6

Dear Johnny,

I hope you don't mind if I call you Johnny. I've known Johnathans and Jonathans and Johns. But never a Johnny. And I'm not comfortable calling you King, sorry. It's kind of nice having a pen pal, though. Sort of feels like we've been old friends for quite a while. I could use a friend about now. My daughter Jen shows no sign of coming back yet.

Thank you for sending Cassie tickets for her birthday. When she opened your letter, she screamed so loud that for a second, I was afraid you really were a creep. Ha! But when she could get her words out (and that gal has a lot of words), she said you sent her the best birthday gift ever, including her bike and the mini-trampoline she got last year. She has managed to injure herself repeatedly on those gifts, and I don't see how she could hurt herself on the tickets. So even though Jen and I don't approve of insults, and Jen doesn't allow her to watch your show I admit I enjoy it. Reminds me of the old-time comedy shows with guys like Groucho Marx and Red Skelton. Mind you, I'm still not fond of the insults. But I don't suppose one live performance can do much harm.

I thought Cassie might try to get her friend Nick to take the second ticket, but I guess that wouldn't have worked out so well, since he's only 11 and can't drive to Hannibal. Then I was sure this would force her to call her mother and offer Jen the ticket. But the day before, we'd heard from Jen that her boss is insisting she keep her speaking commitment at that newspaper convention. So Cassie asked me to go with her. I suppose she was thinking I was her best hope of a ride to Hannibal. And I do like that town and its history.

Looks like we'll be there with bells on!

By the way, I love the names of those towns you've been writing and filming from. Tell your producer that for the next season, your pen pal says he should consider these:

Toad Suck, Arkansas
Lizard Lick, North Carolina
Toadvine, Alabama
Frogtown, Mississippi
Frog City, Illinois
Mousetown, Maryland
Mouse Island, Maine
Squirrel Town, Ohio
Chipmonk, New York

Then the following season:
    Burntfork, Wyoming
    Burnt Cane, Arkansas
    Burnt Cabins, Pennsylvania
    Burnt Chimney Corner, North Carolina
    Burnt Corn, Alabama
    Burnt Creek, Georgia
    Burnt Factory, Virginia and/or West Virginia
        (Yep—there's one in both states.)
    Burnt House, West Virginia
    Burnt Ranch, California
    Burnt Prairie, Illinois
    Burnt Tree, Virginia
    Burnt Woods, Maryland

                        See you soon, Johnny!
                        Emma

From: Travis Barton
Chicago, IL
August 13

To: Jennifer Callahan
San Bernardino, CA

Dear Jen,

I am writing you at this address, which was given
to me by your daughter, Cassie, because I had no
idea you were in San Bernardino until my son,
Nick, told me that. I guess Nick knew because he
and your daughter have remained friends and she
tells him stuff like that, and other things.

    I want you to know that I miss you very, very,
very, very much. Missing you has turned me into a
grump, but I would stop being one if you came back
to me, which is why I am writing you. I know I
could have called you, but you might have hung up
on me. You can't hang up on a letter.

    I don't mind telling you that me leaving with
Julie and Nick was a big, fat mistake, and we are
not happy here in Chicago. For one thing, I don't
like working for Grandad. He was nice to let us
live with him and all, but who really enjoys living
in an old folks' home, except maybe old folks?
Plus, the kids hate the idea of going to the private

school I will make them go to and wear uniforms that will make them look like dorks.

I am very sorry that we left so suddenly, but I couldn't take being rejected again. When you said those things about having doubts about getting married to me and everything, I freaked out, and that explains that. I had a very rough time when my other wife, who is now a ~~movie~~ TV-commercial star, dumped me. I sure didn't want to have to go through that all over again.

I think if you and I could get together again, we could talk it all out and still get married and have our kids be stepbrothers and stepsisters. And we might even end up being a family and living happilyeverafter.

You can call me at the number on the back of this paper, but it wouldn't be a good idea to mention this letter.

Love ya,
Travis

P.S. Nick and Julie miss you very much too. And they miss Cassie and Kirby and even Gram.

From: Jennifer Callahan
San Bernardino, CA
(but I brought this envelope with me, so it looks
like it was postmarked in Hamilton, MO, instead
of San Bernardino)
August 15

To: Travis Barton
Old Folks' Home
Chicago, IL

My dearest Travis,

Even though we haven't seen each other for weeks,
my love for you is unequivocal (which, as you no doubt
know because you are so intelligent, means "absolute;
unqualified; not subject to conditions or exceptions").
So, of course, I miss you very, very, very much, Travis,
my darling. So do Cassie and even Gram.
    I was surprised and hurt when you left so fast
that last night we were together, when your deep
brown eyes grew dark and foreboding, instead of
wide with understanding. But I get it. You were scared,
and sometimes even grown-up men do get scared.
Sometimes they don't, but you did, because you did not
want me to leave you the way your first wife did. And
so, I understand. But I don't think you should have left
and taken Nick and Julie away with you.
    My sweetheart, we should have talked about our
fears together. I, too, was afraid in my own way. I

feared I was betraying my first love, even though he is no longer with us (because he is dead). It is not too late, my love. We can still talk this through like adults (adults who are not so scared that they won't talk to each other). We just need to dialogue with each other.

In my columns, I always say that anything in the house can be cleaned up and fixed if you know how. I think that you and I know how to fix our house. Let us talk.

Come back to Missouri. Or at least write or text. Or, I guess you could even call me, but you'd have to use my cell phone number because I'm not in Hamilton. But let's not say anything about this letter, okay?

Love always,
Jen

P.S. If Cassie and Nick and Julie have been able to stay friends, we should be able to also.

Cassie Callahan
Hamilton, MO
August 15

Dear Jesus,

I guess you saw that letter I wrote to the <u>Last Insult</u>
<u>Standing</u>, huh? It was the best I could do, and I really did
hold back on the mean insults, don't you think? I don't
suppose they'll pick me for that show now, but it would
really help if they did. Nick's trying out too. We both
wanted to win so we could get Travis and Mom on the
same cruise for 10 days. Now I'm thinking that if Nick
wins, he can still count us in as part of his family. Only
right now, that's a stretch. So I guess I better ask you
to come through for us. We need a win. (You said I could
ask you for anything, right?)

Speaking of letters, Nick and I are making this
last-ditch letter-writing effort to our parents, and
we could really use your help. I am writing to Travis
but pretending to be my mom. (Wait—it's for a really
good cause.) Nick is writing Mom, only pretending to be
Travis. We are only saying what they should be saying
to each other, what they WOULD say if they weren't
so messed up right now. Mom is confused because of
how much she loved my dad and doesn't want to be
disloyal to him. (Please say hi to Dad for me. Tell him
I still have his baseball signed by Stan the Man Musial
himself, and it's front and center on my dresser. And
you can tell him that Mom and I still love him, but you

could maybe explain about how even you needed a stepdad down here.)

Travis is all freaked out because of his ex-wife, who just up and left him and little Nick and Baby Julie the second she got an offer to be an actress in Los Angeles. And even though that fell through, she didn't come back home. Not ever. And you know how great Julie and Nick turned out anyway. Their mother is the one missing out, even if she is on a potato-chip commercial.

This letter-writing plan doesn't sound like it's all on the up-and-up, I know. But I'm counting on you knowing what it's like to want your Father. I'll bet you missed your real Father, who stayed up in heaven to run things—but at least he wasn't dead.

My real father is dead, which you know because he's there with you. I know Mom still misses him, and I hope we get to see each other in heaven (only not too soon, okay?). But I miss Travis, too, and he's still down here. Did you miss Joseph, your stepfather? I'm thinking he maybe died when you were young because Mary shows up without him an awful lot.

Gram is only making things worse. She has this habit of humming—and even singing—around the house. This is not a good sound. You would probably still call it a "joyful noise" and be okay with it, but Kirby, our black lab, howls at it. I told Gram about Proverbs 25:20: "Singing cheerful songs to a person with a heavy heart is like taking someone's coat in cold weather or pouring vinegar in a wound." She told me to put a sock in it.

    Thanks for letting me write you about my heavy heart. I know how busy you are, but I still have to keep asking you to get Travis and Mom back together. And I'm hoping you'll help out with the letters Nick and I wrote, and that they'll do the trick. Also it would be great if Nick and I both got to be on <u>The Last Insult Standing</u> and could win that cruise. Even though you probably aren't crazy about some of the insults, could you help out there, too? I really am trying to stay away from mean insults. Pastor Mike says words should build up instead of tearing down, and I'll bet you agree. Only this is not so easy.

Your friend,
Cassie

P.S. Thanks for getting Kirby, King of Insults, to write to me. I think he's got problems of his own. So maybe you could help him out too, when you get time.

Kirby the Insult King
Hog Jaw, AR (just passing through,
thank goodness)

Hey, Kid Callahan,

Remember how I told you about my insult-free little
sister? Well, she died of leukemia when she was only
seven. To tell you the truth, I've been pretty mad
about it ever since. Your not-stepbrother, Nick, sent
me that page you wrote him about the blind guy and
how it wasn't nobody's fault. I was very surprised
when he did that, and I will have to ask him why.
Because that was pretty weird. If you think to ask
him before I get around to it, let me know what the
kid has to say. For years and years, it made me sad
and angry whenever I thought about little Lizzy—
Elizabeth Anne Kirby. But today I thought about
her, and I smiled.

   I got your thank-you card for the tickets. It was
pretty funny. So funny I forgot to laugh.

                                        The King

P.S. That dog of yours—the dog named Kirby—
he, excuse me, she—writes an insulting letter.
It sounds to me like your mutt has been chasing
too many parked cars.

MARTIN SMIRNOFF, PRODUCER
THE LAST INSULT STANDING
NEW YORK, NY
AUGUST 13

Dear Ms. Callahan:

Congratulations!

It is our extreme pleasure to inform you that our judges have selected you as one of our five female finalists in *The Last Insult Standing* contest. Your insults were chosen from hundreds of entries received from all across the United States.

We will be broadcasting the entire contest live from the Mark Twain museum on Main Street in Hannibal, Missouri. You will be expected to report to our production staff by 5 p.m. on August 31.

Please return the enclosed confirmation form and press release, along with the parental consent form, if necessary. We'll see you on August 31!

Once again, hearty congratulations!

Martin Smirnoff, Producer

MARTIN SMIRNOFF, PRODUCER
THE LAST INSULT STANDING
NEW YORK, NY
AUGUST 13

Dear Mr. Barton:

Congratulations!

It is our extreme pleasure to inform you that our judges have selected you as one of our five male finalists in *The Last Insult Standing* contest. Your insults were chosen from hundreds of entries received from all across the United States.

We will be broadcasting the entire contest live from the Mark Twain museum on Main Street in Hannibal, Missouri. You will be expected to report to our production staff by 5 p.m. on August 31.

Please return the enclosed confirmation form and press release, along with the parental consent form, if necessary. We'll see you on August 31!

Once again, hearty congratulations!

Martin Smirnoff, Producer

Cassie Callahan
Hannibal, MO

Dear Nick,

Woohooooo! Yippppeeee! I won!

Cassie

P.S. It's so hard not to tell anybody (but you) that I'm going to be on TV!

P.P.S. How come you sent the King my letter about disease not being anybody's fault? I'm glad you did and everything, but you didn't even know about his sister, did you?

Nick Barton
Chicago, IL

Woohoo! And double yippee! I won too!
    Congratulations!

                                 Love ya,
                              Nick and Julie

P.S. Nick here. I told Julie you won a big contest, but I didn't tell her I won too. And I certainly didn't tell her my plans about getting to Hannibal. But I will see you there!

P.P.S. I didn't know I sent your letter to the Insult King—must have been an accident. I've got all your letters on my desk crammed into Grandad's little den, so I must have stuffed it in when I wrote him. Sorry about that.

Jen Callahan
San Bernardino, CA
August 16

Dear Cassie,

I just received a rather intriguing letter from Chicago, Illinois, claiming to come from Travis. I knew immediately it wasn't from him. And I'd be lying if I told you I'm not embarrassed by it. At first, I thought it had to have come from you somehow, even though the postmark said it was from Chicago. But it did not contain your peculiar vocabulary.

Then I realized it had been written by dear Nick. (Having him call his dad a grump was only one of many clues, others being "love ya" and "old folks' home." Still, it was a very sweet gesture.

I hope you will tell him that I appreciate the time he took to write the letter. And I found it touching and perceptive of him (you may have to explain "perceptive" to him) to have understood his father's reasonable fears. I found that quite surprising, in fact. Didn't know Nick had it in him.

And so, I was amused and, as I said, moved by the letter . . . until I talked with your grandmother this evening.

How could you, Cassie?! Seriously, you actually wrote to Travis? And you pretended you were me? Gram claims she didn't know about your little scheme beforehand. But when I told her about my letter from Nick, she said, "Ah. So that explains it." And she chuckled. Turns out she saw your envelope addressed to Travis, instead of Nick. But she just didn't have time to ask you about it? That's a discussion for another time.

I am mortified that you wrote to Travis on my behalf, impersonating me! I'm horrified to imagine what you must have said! We are going to have a long talk about this very soon, young lady! I would make your grandmother drag you to the phone right now, if I didn't know you were in youth group. You, missy, are in big, big trouble.

Now I have to think what I'm going to do about it.

Love,
Mom

Nick Barton
Chicago, IL
August 18

Dear Cassie,

So, the cat's out of the bag. Or maybe the cat's
still in the bag and at the bottom of the lake. Dad
guessed right away that you were the one who
wrote that letter to him. What did you do wrong,
anyway? Did you use big words or something? He
said you were pretty mushy, which was too much
for somebody who just dumped somebody.

    I'll bet your mom has no idea I wrote the letter
to her.

    But you want to know something funny? Dad
wasn't all that mad. I caught him reading that
letter over and over last night and again this
morning.

Your favorite letter writer,
Nick

P.S. Only 13 more days to Hannibal!

P.P.S. Thanks a million for the extra money. I was
able to book a ticket on a bus that travels at
night, the night of August 30, and it only makes
about one-tenth of the stops the other bus was

going to make. Plus, this one is air-conditioned and has a bathroom right on it.

P.P.P.S. Grandad signed my parental consent form for the live show. (He says if anyone's a parent, it's him.) He hasn't said anything to Dad about it, and I thought he was my partner in crime until I figured out he probably doesn't remember signing the thing. Anyway, I'm taking a copy of it in case the bus driver is awake enough to ask about my age.

TEXT MESSAGE: FROM JEN TO TRAVIS

Jen:

> I feel I must apologize for my daughter. I don't know what she wrote to you. I just know she wrote a letter to you and signed my name, which I suppose you figured out before I did.

Travis:

> No need to apologize. Cassie writes a good letter. And yep, I did realize it wasn't from you the minute she wrote "unequivocal" and then, thankfully, defined it for me.

Jen:

> That's my girl! Nick's letter was pretty good too. He definitely put a lot of thought into it.

Travis:

> Hold on! You mean Nick wrote to you and signed my name?

Jen:

Oops. Sorry—didn't mean to get him in trouble. Actually, it was . . . very thoughtful.

Travis:

I'm going to have a serious talk with that boy. I guess I haven't been doing enough of that lately.

Jen:

I know what you mean.

Travis:

. . .

Jen:

. . .

Johnathan Kirby
The Hour of Insult
Vatican, LA
August 16

Kid Callahan,

Take it easy on your grandmother, kid. Me and Emma
have become pals, and I don't got many of those.

Emma tells me your master plan for getting your
mom and Nick's dad together went south. Sorry about
that, kid. My parents split up when I was about your
age, and it sure ain't no picnic, no matter what
anybody tells you. The one thing I learned was that
it's never the kids' fault. Just so you know.

On a brighter note (man, I never thought I'd say
those words together), I heard you and Nick both are
finalists in The Last Insult Standing. Ain't that
a hoot! I guess after getting letters from the both
of you and getting insulted two ways from Sunday,
I shouldn't be all that surprised. But I wanted
to tell you straight-out that I had nothing to do
with it. I didn't pull no strings. I didn't even get
to see your 10 insults, and I didn't get a vote. Not
that I woulda if I coulda. This contest is all on
the up-and-up legit.

Still,
The King

P.S. Since your grandmother didn't mention to me the fact that you're a finalist, I'm guessing you haven't told her. I won't either. Not my place. But I think you owe it to your gram to tell her you're a contest finalist.

P.P.S. My producer says I haven't been as insulting as usual on my last two shows. This worries me a little. But not too much. I told my producer to put a sock in it.

Callahan the Comic
Hamilton, MO
August 24

Dear Nick,

This time next week we'll be in Hannibal onstage!

You better be careful. I'm getting nervous thinking about you riding a bus all night by yourself. How will you get to the bus station? Do you have enough money for a taxi? How will you get out of the house without Travis stopping you? What if he does? And what's he going to think when he doesn't find you there in the morning and your grandfather doesn't have a clue?

I know you'll get to Hannibal somehow. I can't believe you've never been there. Hannibal's downtown is pretty small, and that's where the museum is. The old museum is next to Samuel Clemens's (Mark Twain's) boyhood home. It's really small, so I'll bet that's why they have tickets. I don't think they can fit that many people in there. Maybe we'll have time to ride the riverboat down the Mississippi River. You can walk to everything—that's how small downtown is.

Only I don't know where the bus station is. If I had a cell phone, you could call me when you get in. But Gram has a phone, and you have that number. So use it! And if she doesn't answer, she's probably turned off her ringer. But you could still text her, and I'll make sure she checks her phone a lot. So text her the second your bus pulls into the Hannibal station, and we'll come and pick you up—even though she will be surprised that you're there. All of this is not easy to keep straight.

Insultingly yours,
Cassie

Nick Barton
Old Folks' Home
Chicago, IL
August 28

Dear Cassie,

There may be a small audience in the museum, but the television audience will be huge. I admit I'm getting a little worried about it. Do you remember when I had to give that book report to our class and I couldn't remember anything, not even the title of the book? Kids started laughing, and that made it worse. Then I saw you, and you grabbed your neck and stuck out your tongue like you were gagging or being strangled . . . or poisoned. The book was called <u>Poison</u>! And that was what I needed to get through that report, which I did, even though I puked in the hall afterward.

    Maybe you better be ready to act out some insults so I don't just stand there.
    See you SOON!

Signed,
Nervous Nick

Friday Morning Phone Call

Phone: *Ring! Ring!*

Jen: Hello?

Gram: Jen, this is your mother.

Jen: I recognize your voice, Mom. And your phone number on caller ID. Is everything all right? Nothing's wrong with Cassie, is there? Are you—?

Gram: Why would anything be wrong?

Jen: Because I just got up and I'm not thinking straight, and you haven't said why you're calling and what this is about.

Gram: It's nine o'clock in the morning, Jen. How can you sleep in like that and still keep your job?

Jen: It's 7 a.m. here, Mom. Time difference. Remember? What's the problem?

Gram: More like *who* is the problem.

Jen: Fine. Who?

Gram: Johnathan Kirby, in a way.

Jen: Ha. Like the Insult King?

Gram: Exactly like the Insult King.

Jen: What are you talking about?

Gram: Who. And I guess it's more about Cassie really. I did call about Cassie.

Jen: Cassie? What's wrong? Did something happen to her? Is she—?

Gram: Cassie is fine. Super, in fact. She won a contest.

Jen: She did? What kind of contest? Why didn't I know she even entered a contest?

Gram: Because you're in California, and Cassie is here, in Hamilton, Missouri.

Jen: . . .

Gram: Actually, she's not the winner yet. But she's one of five female finalists in the contest. We have tickets to see the show. Johnny got them for us.

Jen: Johnny? Johnny who?

Gram: Kirby, the King. We're friends. Anyway, Cassie believed that I thought we were just going to watch the contest. But I had already read the letter congratulating her on being a finalist. I figured she'd let me know when she wanted me to know. And she did. When she finally broke the news to me, I pretended to be surprised. Then I signed her parental consent form.

Jen: Wait. I'm having trouble taking this all in, Mom. Cassie's a finalist in a contest that you're going to watch. Where? Where are you going? And when? And what kind of contest? And seriously, *Johnny*?

Gram: We'll be leaving for Hannibal early in the morning. More like the middle of the night.

Jen: But . . . you mean *tomorrow* morning? Cassie's birthday? You still haven't told me what the contest is about.

Gram: Insults.

Jen: *Groan.*

Gram: I have to go now, Jen. You should come home. Cassie needs her mother.

Jen: But I can't. Not now. I have that speech to give tomorrow. And this week's column to write. Mom? Mom? *Mom?*

Gram: *Click.*

Cassie Callahan
Between Hamilton and Hannibal, MO
August 31

Dear Julie,

I hope you're doing better. I feel lousy that Nick and I had to keep something this big from you. It had to be a secret, though. Only by the time you get this, it will all be over anyway. And with any luck, we'll all be on a cruise ship heading to the Bahamas.

Let me explain. In fact, I'm writing you a live, as-it-happens report of everything you'll be missing here. Since you can't be in Hannibal, I will bring Hannibal to you! When you get this, the cat will be out of the bag. I'm guessing your dad will call my gram as soon as he discovers Nick is missing. Nick will be in big trouble, but at least you won't be because we've kept you out of it on purpose (even though we both hated doing that).

For the record, Nick and I are finalists in The Last Insult Standing contest to be held tomorrow evening (make that THIS evening, which means "Happy Birthday to me!") at the Mark Twain museum in Hannibal, Missouri. We have to compete—me with four other insulting females, and Nick with four insulting males. The guy winner will have to face the girl winner. And then the big winner gets a cruise for the whole family, and that's why we're doing this, Julie, so that ALL of us can be a family for at least 10 days, on a ship, where nobody can run away. One of us just has to win.

It's so early in the morning that it's still dark, and I've been writing by the dome light and sitting in the backseat while Gram squints at Old Highway 36 and drives 30 miles an hour so we won't hit any deer. She doesn't like the new highway, so it's going to take forever to get to Hannibal.

Only now I have to stop writing because she says she can't see well with the light on inside the car. Plus, I'm getting carsick.

To be continued . . .
Cassie

SHOPPING LIST

Dad, if you're reading this, it's probably Saturday morning, and you don't realize that I'm not still in bed. Or maybe Julie got up first, read this note, woke you up, and now you're reading it.

Or maybe (and I hope this isn't the right one) you checked on me in the middle of the night like you do sometimes— yep, I've heard you come into my room and just stare at me while I'm pretending to be asleep. Why do I pretend? Because I kind of like that you peek in on me. Only you haven't done

SHOPPING LIST

that since we moved to Chicago.

So back to now. ~~have won that contest~~ I am one of five guys who are finalists on <u>The Last Insult Standing</u>. There are also five girl finalists, of which Cassie is one. If I win the whole thing, I win a cruise for the entire family, 10 days on the ocean and in the Bahamas and other countries I can't remember the names of. And I thought it would only be fair to let Cassie and her family come along as part of my family because it still does feel like she is. And her mom and Gram.

SHOPPING LIST

I need to win this contest. You wouldn't take me to Hannibal when I asked you to, so I have to take the bus. I am sorry if I'm making you crazy and worried, but I'm fine. I'm probably still on the very fancy and comfortable bus that takes me all the way to Hannibal, Missouri, where the contest is. And if you want to, you and Julie can watch me on TV tomorrow (probably now today) evening at seven o'clock, same channel as The Hour of Insult.

Before you try to call me on my cell and yell at me, you should know that I've turned off the ringer so I can

SHOPPING LIST

sleep on the bus and not get yelled at before I compete in the contest, and turning off your phone is probably a bus rule anyways. But the main reason is that I don't want to hear you yell at me until this contest is over and we are on the cruise, because I don't think you will feel like yelling then.

Love ya,
Nick

P.S. Tell Julie that I wish she could have come with me. She did not know anything about this. So don't take it out on her. I'll be back.

Cassie continuing . . .

Hey, Julie—I'm back! And we're in Hannibal, Missouri! As usual, Gram had us here hours early. But this was early, even for Gram, who has always been first in the pick-up line at school (by about 30 minutes at least) and who freaks out when she's just on time or only a few minutes early.

But I didn't mind at all this time. We got to visit Mark Twain's home, even though it didn't open to the public until later. And we got a personal tour of the downtown area, including the Mark Twain museum and the riverboat on the Mississippi River! Who gave us this grand tour? Kirby the Insult King!

You should have heard Gram when she called the King to let him know we'd arrived. They sounded like school chums (that's an old-time, Gram word for "friends"), and the King said he'd be right over. I asked Gram if she'd like to put on lipstick to meet him. She laughed. Me too. I'm glad she's not one of those grandmothers who pile on red lipstick and cake blue eye shadow and eyeliner in thick, jagged lines.

The King got here fast and used his own key to unlock Mark Twain's house, and we walked through it together. When we finally got outside again, I plopped onto this park bench to soak up the sun and cool breeze from the river. Flowers are blooming everywhere, and do they ever smell stupendous and phenomenal (haven't used my words much this week).

I spy an inordinate (yep, word for today) number of cardinals flying around. Sounds like they're tweeting, "Happy Birthday to Cassie!"

I sure wish Nick would hurry up and get here!

To be continued . . .

Phone call to Emma Hendren from Travis
Barton

Phone: *Ring! Ring! Ring!*

Travis [muttering under breath]: Answer your
phone, Emma!

King Kirby: What's that buzzing sound? I think
it's coming from your purse. You expecting a
call?

Gram: I don't hear anything.

Phone: *Buzz! Buzz!*

Phone call from Jen Callahan to Emma Hendren

Phone: *Ring! Ring! Ring!*

Jen [muttering under breath]: Come on, Mom!
Pick up, will you?

Gram: I'm starving. Got anything to eat around
here, Johnny?

King Kirby: Follow me.

Cassie: Gram, can I see your phone? Thanks.
Okay. It's not Nick.

Gram: Why would Nick be calling me?

Phone: *Ring! Ring! Ring!*

Gram's phone: *You have reached the voice mail of Emma Hendren. Please leave a message after the beep.*

Jen: Where are you? I've been calling the house and your cell. Listen, Mom, you were right. Cassie needs me. I don't want to miss her big moment. I'm in the airport right now. I should arrive in Kansas City this afternoon. Then I'll rent a car and drive to Hannibal. Tell Cassie I'm on my way!

Phone call from Travis to Emma

Phone: *Ring! Ring! Ring!*

Travis [muttering under breath]: She's not picking up! What's the matter with her?

Gram: I haven't had this many calls since I burned a pan of cinnamon rolls and set off the smoke alarm, and the fire department came to put out the fire in my oven.

King Kirby: Emma, you make me laugh! You and the kid both.

Phone: *Ring! Ring! Ring!*

Julie: Leave a message this time, Dad! You have to go!

Gram's phone: *You have reached the voice mail of Emma Hendren. Please leave a message after the beep.*

Travis: Emma, I wish you'd answer your phone! Nick's run off. He's taken a bus, but I don't know which one. I know he means to get to Hannibal, so I'm taking the first flight there and renting a car. I'm leaving Julie with Dad and his housekeeper. From Nick's note, it sounds like Cassie's going to Hannibal too. If you see Nick, tell him—

Gram's phone: *End of voice mail. To listen to your message, press . . .*

TEXT TO GRAM FROM NICK:

Nick:

> Gram, are you there? I'm here! In the bus station. Can you come get me?? It's kind of creepy here.

To Julie, continued . . .
Hannibal, MO

Hey, Julie!

We've got Nick!

   We almost didn't. I'd warned him that if he called
Gram, he shouldn't leave a voice mail because she
doesn't know how to retrieve messages. She's had the
ringer off since we got here. So Nick sent Gram
a text. And, of course, Gram didn't hear the text
come in. She was too busy eating donuts. But I started
getting worried about Nick, so I asked Gram to check
her text messages. She did, and there he was! He'd
been waiting at the bus station for over an hour. So
Mr. Kirby drove us there to pick him up. And that was
pretty nice for an insult king. He tried to phone your
dad, and so did Gram, but they never got him. Gram
couldn't believe your dad wasn't driving Nick here.

   The bus station isn't anything to write home about.
Two old guys were sleeping on the concrete floor, and
a group of guys who looked like they could star in a
gangland-murder movie rated R were laughing like crazy
and kept looking over at Nick. When Nick saw us, he
came running. "You came! You're here!" he cried. I have a
feeling he won't be traveling alone again anytime soon.

   Nick's pretty wrinkly since he slept on the bus in his
clothes. He kind of smells bad too, like the old Geri's
Tavern on Main Street in Hamilton. Remember? We used

to have to walk past it to get to Dairy Dan's. Nick said the guy next to him on the bus kept pulling out a silver metal bottle (which is called a flask, although Nick didn't say that word). Sometime during the night, the bus stopped fast and the guy spilled his whiskey flask all over Nick. Your brother didn't bring anything else to wear, so he went into the bus bathroom and tried to wash his shirt and wash off his pants, which are still kind of damp and smelly.

Kirby offered to buy Nick a new shirt and pants, which was also pretty nice for an insult king. (You would not believe how nice the king is to Gram and how nice she is back. Just like old buddies.) But Nick said no thanks because there's nothing he hates more than shopping for clothes. The Insult King has to drive us—

Nick just asked me what I'm writing about. When I told him I'm writing you, he said, "For crying out loud, you numskull, will you just get a cell phone?" So I guess he's in good insult shape for our contest.

I don't think I'm in good shape for the contest at all. I didn't even insult him back or make fun of the way he smells, which is still a lot like that tavern.

I have been reading Proverbs in the Bible all week. Some of those proverbs I've read so many times that I have them memorized, Julie. You know how easy it is for things to stick to my brain and get stuck in my head— like songs and commercials and words and definitions. Anyway, with those proverbs stuck there, I just haven't been feeling all that insulting, not even when I think of Mom being in California on my birthday without me. Not even when I think about Travis just leaving like he did, without even saying good-bye to somebody who was almost his stepkid and who thought of him as Dad already because he was the closest thing to it she could remember.

So I'm hoping the insults come back to me here, like riding a bicycle, which I'm not so great at, so maybe that's not the best analogy (word of the day, which means "a similarity between like features of two things, on which a comparison may be based"). (See what I mean about things sticking to my brain?)

We are back in town now, and Nick is asking me a thousand questions.

More later . . .

Later: Cassie to Julie
Hannibal, MO
Still August 31

Hi, Julie,

In case you're wondering, I really like writing you about everything. It's kind of like when I used to journal because our teacher made us. Only this is better because no one is making me and because it's you instead of me at the other end of this letter.

The King and Gram sent Nick and me back to the boyhood home of Samuel Clemens, aka Mark Twain. King Kirby told me to "show the kid around" because the tourist stuff is now open for business. Gram objected and said we were too young to be on our own, but the Insult King said, "Are you kidding? Nick smells so bad, he'd make skunks run away. The government could use him as a lethal weapon. Nobody will bother them!" And Gram laughed.

Nick and I walked the sidewalks, which are lined with those tiny white flowers you love. They've got big pots of flowers on the corners, with marigolds, zinnias, phlox, and other flowers I don't know the names of but that smell so good you can even smell them when you're walking next to Nick.

You probably guessed that Nick isn't much of a sightseer. We zoomed through the boyhood home and headed to the museum so Nick could scope out the

148

stage and everything. But there's still a curtain closed onstage, so we couldn't see much.

Right now we're sitting in the auditorium of the Mark Twain museum, and it's all I can do to keep Nick here, instead of letting him go and peek behind the curtain. It's like a little theater here, and the cameras and TV monitors and crew of The Hour of Insult take up half of the room. No wonder people had to buy tickets for The Last Insult Standing. It will be standing room only—haha! I'll bet they can't fit more than 50 people in here, which is a good thing because I'm nervous enough as it is.

Julie, I wish you were here! It's great to see Nick again—don't get me wrong. But Nick is so psyched about the contest that he keeps insulting me, head to toe:

HEAD:

"Cassie never got a brain. They only handed them out to people who would use them."

"Come on, Cassie. Use your head! It's the little things that count."

"Poor Cassie. I had to explain to her that a quarterback is not a refund and a jungle gym isn't Tarzan's little brother."

"Cassie's so spacey, she asked me to go see a movie

after she saw it advertised on a sign outside our local theater. I asked her the name of the movie, and she said, 'THEATER CLOSED FOR THE SEASON.'"

TOE:

"Cassie, your feet are so big, you'd be disqualified from the swim meet for wearing flippers."

"You caught athlete's foot because you thought it would make you run faster."

"Cassie's toenails are so long, she cuts the grass by walking barefoot."

"Cassie's feet are so big that when we were walking around Hannibal before the show, she got pulled over by a cop, who asked for their license and registration."

Nick can't understand why I'm not insulting him back, and I'm not exactly sure myself. It's hard to explain. He knows I've been writing to Jesus and everything. But he still doesn't quite get it. You'd get it—I know you would. I guess I've been learning that words have power. Does that sound crazy? I've always liked words. I just didn't realize how powerful they are—for good or bad. And the truth is—

Oops—gotta run!

Later

Oh my goodness! Julie, this is crazy weird! I should have known it, but I didn't, and neither did Nick, because he's kind of freaking out. ALL of the other contestants are grown-ups! Nick and I are the only kids! Three of the women are gorgeous! And the other one looks funny, like a comedian.

One of the producers of <u>The Last Insult Standing</u> rounded us up (which is why I had to leave you in the middle of a sentence). They moved us to the "greenroom," which isn't green at all, but just a smaller room with a table and 10 chairs for us, the finalists. The lady producer introduced us, and the other contestants did double takes when she got to Nick and me. "I know," she said. "Yes, they're contestants, just like you."

I think they thought they were being teased, or insulted. Even when we left the room, I think half of them still thought we were a joke. One of the gorgeous women contestants came up to me and said, "Are you sure you're not that producer's daughter?" I don't think she believed me when I told her I wasn't.

Now even Nick is more nervous than he is excited.

Here's how the whole thing is supposed to work, according to that producer. The "men" will be going first (kind of an insult to the ladies right off). All five men stand onstage at little pedestals, like on the presidential debates you and Nick and I watched with Mom and Travis and Gram at our house, when we popped popcorn and drank homemade slushies. Contestant #1 starts off with an insult to Contestant #2 (which is also like in the presidential debates). Contestant #2 responds to that insult, then turns to Contestant #3 and insults him. Contestant #3 responds to that, then turns to Contestant #4 and insults him. And so on with #5. That's Round 1. Then the judges (three of them, famous adult comedians I haven't heard of) tell one man to go home. Then the four contestants still onstage go through the whole insult chain all over again. After Round 2, another contestant is told to get lost, and the three left go at it. And so on, until only two men (or hopefully, one man and one boy) remain.

Then it's the girls' turn.

The female contestants will come onstage and go through their rounds until they get down to the last two ladies (hopefully, one lady, one girl). Then it's back to the men, with the two male finalists competing onstage to see who will be the Last Male Insult Standing.

After that, the two female finalists compete for the Last Female Insult Standing. And finally, the girl champ faces the boy champ, and the winner takes the family to the Bahamas. We just have to win!

Nick was so shook up that he didn't get any of what the producer was saying. So I just showed him what I wrote to you about how we'll play the insult game. Now, he's muttering insults.

And I can't think of a single one!

Julie! Can't write more!
   Nick is onstage with the other male contestants.
   AND Travis just walked in!!!!

Round I is over! Judges are conferring (word of the day last week, means "consulting together, discussing, deliberating, comparing opinions").
   Nick did great, though. The guy next to him said, "You're so fat that when you get your shoes shined, you have to take their word for it." (And Nick isn't fat and only wears tennis shoes—duh). So Nick turned to the audience and said, "You'll have to pardon Cliff here. He signed up for the Ugly Contest next door, and they turned him down because they can't take professionals." Everybody laughed, especially one of the judges.
   This waiting is killing me! Cameras are everywhere, and I—

He made it! Nick survived Round I! (Cliff had to go home!)

Julie, sorry! We're up to Round 3, and Nick is still in! Travis is sitting right next to me. He saw that I've been writing you, so he says hi, he loves you, and he's really sorry he couldn't bring you because he had to pay a fortune for even one ticket to fly here last minute.

Waiting for the judges to send someone home again. Travis and I agree that Nick did the best job. I thought the other two guys had to resort to old insults. Bet you've heard all of them:

"You're not the sharpest knife in the drawer."

"I don't want to make a monkey out of you. Why should I take all the credit for the one thing you've done yourself?"

"I don't exactly hate you, but if you were on fire and I had water, I'd drink it."

"You're so fat you get clothes in three sizes: extra large, jumbo, and oh-my-gosh-it's-coming-toward-us!" (Again, Nick is so not fat!)

Nick came back with:

Nick: "Excuse me. Fat? Pay attention, dude! Don't let your mind wander. It's way too small to be let out on its own."

Dude: "You're a knucklehead, and I'd say a lot more if you weren't a kid."

Nick: "Okay. It's really not what you say, sir. It's the thought behind it that counts. Unfortunately, apparently there is no thought whatsoever behind anything you've said so far."

Nick cracked up the crowd after the snootiest contestant said something really rude, which I won't write down. Nick acted like he was shocked and told the guy, "No! Don't look at the audience!" The guy turned to Nick, and Nick said, "Phew! Don't want them to think it's Halloween."

Julie! They just announced the final two male contestants—drumroll! Mike Something and NICK BARTON! Nick made it! And his insults weren't even mean. They were really nice compared to the others. You should hear Travis. He's hurting my ears. So is Gram. Travis is jumping up and waving his arms. Nick can't help grinning. He was saying he hasn't seen Travis smile in weeks. Woo-hoo!! Is Travis ever smiling now!

Wait. The Insult King is coming out and congratulating Mike and Nick. Now he's sending them to the audience, telling them they'll have to wait until the ladies have their turn.

Yikes! That's me! My turn!

Dear Julie,

This is Nick here. I knew Cassie was writing you while I was onstage. I'm glad. You should be here! Hope you got my note and understood why I couldn't tell you everything. You're not a good liar, and I had to get here, Jules.

Can you believe Dad? He's not even all that mad at me, although that will probably come later. He screamed louder than anybody when I was onstage. I can't believe I've made it to the Finals. I just hope I can beat that guy, Mike. And I really hope Cassie beats all the "ladies." If we both win, then we have to insult each other. But by then, it wouldn't matter who won. We'd get the family cruise.

No way!
This is even better than we planned! Cassie's mom just walked in—ran in—dodging the ticket-taking guy. Dad had to rush over and help her because the security guard was going to carry her out of here. Then Gram ran over, and I thought she was going to kick that security guy. Then Kirby the Insult King got in on it and said something to the security guard, and they let Jen come in.

Cassie hasn't even seen her mom yet because they closed the big red curtain, and she's behind it with the four ladies. Wow, will she be surprised! But the lights are so bright up onstage, Cassie might not be able to see her mom in the audience.

I couldn't see Dad for a long time. And when I did, I still couldn't believe my eyes.

The curtain's opening! Cassie is standing in the middle, but you can't see her because she's so short. Now Kirby's coming onstage (because Gram hollered something up to him). A guy in a T-shirt and holey jeans is dragging out a step stool, and Cassie's getting up on it behind her podium. Okay. Now we can see her. I was so scared up there onstage, but Cassie looks calm and cool as a cucumber, which is funny because why are cucumbers so calm? A lot of them end up as pickles.

The Insult King is introducing everybody to the audience. Megan, the first lady, has straight red hair that goes down to her waist, and she's wearing a bright red dress. I don't want to take time to tell you what the others are wearing, though. Cassie is Cassie—jeans and her Beatles T-shirt, hair in a ponytail. The last female contestant—I think the King said her name is Sharon—is big, as in round. She'll probably get all the fat jokes.

I have to admit something. When that guy kept saying I was fat, it made me feel like hiding behind the curtain—and I'm not even fat. Made me feel bad for Noah, you know, the kid in my class who never plays soccer or softball at recess. And if he did, he'd get picked last for a team. He gets teased for being overweight, even when he's just watching us play. I've never teased him

. . . but I've laughed when Aiden and Connor did.
I won't laugh anymore.

They're starting . . .

Man, it's hard to keep up. End of Round 1, and I
think Cassie did great. But to tell the truth, she
didn't fit with the others. I mean, like, some
of what she said was over my head, but that's
always true with her big words, I guess.

The other contestants said things like (and Gram
and Jen are helping me write this now):

"You're so stupid, you jumped off a boat and
missed the water."

"I'll bet it takes you two hours to watch
60 Minutes." (Gram says 60 Minutes is a TV news
show that's been on forever.)

"Your face looks like it caught on fire and
someone tried to put it out with a hammer."

I think the "ladies" are meaner than the "men."

Except for Cassie. She started out with:

"When arguing with a stupid person, just be sure
she isn't doing the same."

When Sharon called her stupid, Cassie just smiled
and said, "Stupid is as stupid does." Sharon frowned
like Cassie was dangerously crazy. Cassie went on:
"I'm just sayin', if you can't talk without insulting
someone, you might try not talking at all."

Sharon said more mean stuff and called Cassie
stupid again. Cassie said, "My mom says you can fix
anything around the household with duct tape. But

even duct tape won't fix stupid . . . although it might muffle the sound of it if properly placed."

That one got a huge laugh from the audience, which seemed to make Sharon really mad.

Then the redhead insulted Cassie, and when the audience groaned, Red said little Cassie can take it because she's a "mature child." Grinning, Cassie said, "'Mature child' is an oxymoron, ma'am, like 'a fine mess' or 'absolutely unsure' or 'awfully pretty' or 'accidentally on purpose' or 'horribly funny.' Get it? An oxymoron." Sharon looked confused and demanded, "Did you just call me a moron?"

See what I mean about Cassie being kind of confusing? I just hope she got enough laughs to get her to Round 2.

She made it! Cassie's still in!

Sorry, Julie. I'm so nervous I've been bad about writing. It's Round 2, and I forgot everything the other contestants said. Cassie has said stuff like:

"A sharp tongue does not necessarily indicate a sharp mind."

"I find your comments censorious, contumelious, defamatory, derisive, and disparaging, if not insolent, scurrilous, vilifying, and downright vituperative." (Dad helped me with the list. Gram, too. And Jen. But we probably left out some. Only Cassie . . .)

The redhead was really awful and mean, not funny at all. Cassie just said, "My grandma always says it's better to let someone think you're a loser than to open your mouth and prove it," which is kind of like what Mark Twain said: "It is better to keep your mouth shut and appear stupid than to open it and remove all doubt."

Here it comes—she made it! Round 3. It's Sharon, the redhead called Megan, and Cassie!

I admit I was afraid Cassie would be sent home on that one. Guess the judges have a big vocabulary too. One more round, and she'll be in the finals like me!

Round 3, and I really don't know where Cassie's going with this. Sharon and the redhead are throwing out tough and funny insults. Cassie is not. She has her comebacks. They're one-liners. Weird-funny, but not insulting. Sharon seemed to get angrier and angrier. She took up half of Cassie's time with a string of foul insults. So Cassie stared right at her and said: "A truly wise person uses few words; a person with understanding is even-tempered."

It was the redhead's turn after that, but she acted like she'd been hit between the eyes. She had no comeback. I'm thinking she may be the one sent home (if it's not Cassie).

I'm right! Cassie is in the finals with Sharon, the round woman! I can't stand it! If she can beat Sharon—

To Julie, continued . . .

Hey, Julie. Cassie here. I'm back. And so is Mom!

I could not believe it when I saw her. I couldn't see anything from the stage, not with all the lights and TV cameras. So when I left the stage and came down to sit with Nick and Gram, there she was. Mom was crying. But it was the good kind of happy cry. She ran up the aisle and hugged me so hard I couldn't breathe. And I hugged her back as hard as I could. She ditched her newspaper conference and flew all night to get here. Then she had to rent a car and drive. She did all of that just to see me in the contest!

I haven't asked Mom if she's going back to San Bernardino to keep looking for herself, or if maybe she could just look here, in Missouri. If we can win the cruise, I think she'll have to stay, don't you?

I keep looking over at Mom to make sure she's still here. She is. She's talking to Gram. But she and Travis aren't looking at each other. They're both smiling and acting all happy and everything, but they're not saying much to each other. They would have to talk on the cruise! Nobody could run away, not in the middle of the ocean.

Wasn't Nick great to pick up where I left off in this journal? I thumbed through some of the pages he wrote, and he missed a lot. I'll fill you in later. Your dad says he's calling you the minute this contest is over.

It was so weird being onstage. All I could think of was that stuff about making sure words are wholesome and filled with grace. Then I just couldn't bring myself to insult like I usually do.

You know, I was ready with a bunch of put-down one-liners, filled with sarcasm and meanness, because I want to win. But each time I started on an insult, the words of a proverb popped into my mind and shoved the meanness out of my head and the proverb out of my mouth.

Mom just came back over to sit by me. "Cassie," she said, "I'm very proud of you." I wanted to say thanks, but I couldn't get it out, because I had to swallow tears. Mom hates insults, but she's proud of me.

"Stand up," she said. She stood up first. "I need another birthday hug."

I stood up and hugged her. Then a very cool thing happened. Your dad appeared and hugged me too. So I was sandwiched, kind of squished between the two of them, and it felt really great. Then Nick squirmed between them too, and made it a four-way birthday hug. Then Gram got in on the action. I know we were each wishing you were here in the center of the hug, where you belong.

Mom and Travis still love each other, Julie. And they both love us—you and me and Nick.

"Ladies and gentlemen!" Kirby the Insult King is calling us to order. (Actually, he's telling us to shut up.) "Mike and Nick will now enter the male insult finals, where insults can fly freely back and forth."

Nick looks okay up there now. But you should have seen him when I came back and sat down, and he had to go back up onstage. I think he forgot that the male finalists have to compete before the female finalists. Mr. Kirby called Nick and Mike to the stage, and Mike was up there cheering for himself for a few minutes, while Nick sat frozen to his seat. Travis almost carried him out to the aisle.

Can you believe that both Nick and I have made it this far? Man, I hope Nick wins. I don't see how I can beat Sharon, but I'll bet Nick could. Don't get me wrong—I'll try my best. But something's changed in me. Insults aren't so automatic.

Okay. Nick's up there with Mike now! I'll try to write down what the last two male finalists, of which Nick is one, say. But it won't be easy. This time, in this final round, they get to go back and forth at each other however they like. Here goes!

Mike: Nick here is such an idiot, he failed a taste test.

Nick: Mike returned a dozen donuts to the store . . . because they all had holes in them.

Mike: Are you always this stupid, kid? Or are you making a special effort today?

Nick: At least I'm honest. Mike here steals free samples at the grocery store. And he snuck a big spoon into the Super Bowl.

Mike (who looks like he's getting angry): You really are a nut job, Nick. But I guess brains aren't everything. In fact, in your case, they're nothing.

Nick (who looks like he's enjoying himself): Well, I would never say Mike is crazy . . . but during the break he asked me what comes after X. I said, "Y," and he swore at me and said, "Because I want to know, kid!" The closest this guy gets to a brainstorm is a light drizzle.

Mike: Oh yeah? Well, if you ever want to lose 10 pounds, I'll happily chop off your head!

Nick (looking up): Mike, do you ever wonder if clouds look down at us and say, "There! Doesn't that one look like a kid?" And, "That one's shaped like a jerk!"

Mike: You little—! (Mike said three quick insults, which I won't repeat, because they're just too nasty. Most of the audience laughed hard, though. I did not.)

That's when the buzzer sounded. And the audience kept roaring with laughter at Mike's insults.
 Travis, Mom, Gram, and I are just sitting here, waiting. And waiting.

Julie, why is it taking them so long to decide? Poor Nick looks lost up there onstage.

Here comes the Insult King. He's taking slips of paper, the ballots, from each of the judges. He's going to announce the winner of the Last Male Insult Standing.

"And the winner, who will face the winner of the ladies' insult contest, is . . ."

Not Nick.

Nick didn't win. I think I already knew it. Not because Nick didn't do great, but I could tell by the way Kirby walked to the microphone, like he didn't want to be the one delivering this bad news.

This is awful. Nick is out. Now it's all up to me. And if I don't win . . .

Nick the Loser here.

I lost, Julie. I wish you were here to give me one of your bear hugs and tell me it's okay and you're still proud of your big brother. I really thought I had it sewn up . . . until Mike hit me with rapid-fire insults right at the end. Of course, he used words Dad would have killed me for using.

Jen and Gram and Dad are being really nice, which is what people are to losers. Cassie punched me in the arm, hard, before she left to go onstage. Somehow, that was the best, like her punch said it was okay and I was still Nick, not a big loser, and she didn't feel sorry for me.

But now I've put all the pressure on her. It's up to Cassie. I feel bad about that. All along, I've been picturing this contest. I've imagined that Cassie and I would both win, and we'd end up in the finals. But it's weird. That's where my vision ended. I've had trouble imagining Cassie and me insulting each other for real. I know. We've insulted each other ever since the first day we met. But, well, I don't know. Insults don't seem all they're cracked up to be today. (Did I just insult insults?)

Maybe that's because I'm a big, fat loser (who isn't fat).

Oh man! Cassie is on her little step onstage, and Sharon looks like she's ready to gobble Cassie up for lunch. My hand is shaking too much to write.

Hi, Julie. Gram here. I reckon I'd better take over, since Nick looks like he can barely hold on to the pen. The show has cut to another commercial break, so I'll try to catch you up.

I hope you're doing okay, honey. I sure do miss you. You'd be mighty proud of your brother and almost stepsister. Those two are really something!

We all wish you were here, sugar! Even Johnny (the Insult King) asked where you were. Who would have thought he'd end up as a friend? Life sure has a way of surprising us, doesn't it?

Oh my! They're back. Onstage, it's that mean gal, Sharon, and our little Cassie.

Johnathan Kirby turns to us, the audience, and says, "We're here for the final female round to determine the Last Female Insult Standing. I'd like to give a special welcome to the families of our contestants."

He means us, and the cameras shift to get us on TV. I feel my cheeks heat up in a big ol' blush. Julie, did you ever hear what Mark Twain said about blushing? He said, "Man is the only animal that blushes. Or needs to." Ha!

Now Johnny is staring into the camera as if he's confiding to his TV audience. "Everybody here brings me a lot of joy," he says, "when they leave." Ha ha. "And now, Sharon and Cassie, it's time to insult!"

Sharon: I'm glad it's you up here, kid, because I've got a message for you: children should never be seen or heard or born! And here's another message for you—stop smiling! W. C. Fields said to start off every day with a smile and get it over with. You should be over it by now.

Cassie: You brought me two messages? There's a proverb that says, "Trusting a fool to convey a message is like cutting off one's feet or drinking poison."

Sharon: You think you're so smart with your little proverbs. Well, here's one for you: respect your elders! Ain't you never heard that one, kid? Honor your elders, or something?

Cassie (smiling sweetly): "Honoring a fool is as foolish as tying a stone to a slingshot."

Sharon: I can't even understand you! (She's getting really mad now!)

Sharon: *x!@#$$(&^%#$

Julie, I just can't keep up with that gal's meanness! She's not just insulting our Cassie. She's calling her names! Cassie is sticking with her one-liners and her proverbs, and it's pushing that woman over the edge. Why, I'd like to

Nick here! Julie, Gram got so mad at Sharon for swearing at Cassie that she started storming out of her seat and heading for the stage. Dad's calming her down now, but I'll try to keep you up to date.

Sharon is still shouting at Cassie, like Cassie's really getting to her. "You little twerp!" she says. And she's saying other words that probably come out as BLEEP BLEEP on television because they can't say those words on regular TV. I don't know why the audience is laughing. The names she's calling Cassie are not funny. Now she's getting right in Cassie's face. "You think you're so smart with your big words!" she shouts. I can see spit flying. I hope it misses Cassie.

Cassie says real sweet, "I'm just sayin'. Wise words satisfy like a good meal."

Sharon, looking confused and angry, says, "Are you calling me fat?" She doesn't wait for an answer, but keeps going off on Cassie like you wouldn't believe. There is nothing funny about anything she's saying. She's out of control and crazy mad! I want this to be over!

"Didn't anybody tell you that you're just a kid?" Sharon says. "A runt of a kid at that. You ought to eat spinach and grow big and strong enough to tell your ma you won't eat the stuff."

The buzzer went off. I don't think any of us knows how Cassie did. But we're all super proud of her. I hope she knows that.

Now we wait.

And wait.

Julie, Dad just took Jen's hand, and she didn't pull away or anything. They both look as scared as I feel. Gram does too.

Here comes Kirby the Insult King. He's talking with those three judges. I think he's arguing with them. Now he's walking toward the microphone to announce the winner, the Last Female Insult Standing.

I lost.

This is me, Cassie. Nick threw this letter down on the ground and stomped it when Kirby announced that Sharon was the winner. That's why this page is so wrinkly.

Yep. Sharon won. When Mr. Kirby read out her name, Sharon was the only one in the whole auditorium who cheered. The room grew as still as a snow-covered Hamilton night. You could have heard a sledgehammer drop, as Gram likes to say. And all of this is on live TV. I'll bet people all over America are still fiddling with their TVs, thinking something's wrong with their cable volume.

They cut for a commercial. King Kirby came offstage and headed for us. He didn't look any happier than we did. "I'm sorry, kids," he said in a tone that was about as far from an insult as you can get. "I tried to talk sense into those judges, but they wouldn't budge. I can't change their minds."

"This isn't your fault," Gram said. "We'll be fine."

Nick took it really hard. "Can we go home now?" he asked Kirby. "I don't want to hear Sharon and Mike insult each other. I've had my fill of insults."

"Me too." I was trying not to cry, but the tears were in my voice, so I cleared my throat. "Mr. Kirby, thank you for everything. Thanks for writing me back, finally. And for showing us around Hannibal and everything." I wanted to make him feel better, so I said, "Nick and I want you to know that this really has been fun. Mostly. In fact, we agree with Groucho Marx, who said: 'I've had a perfectly wonderful evening. But this wasn't it.'"

The King started to say something, but his producer grabbed his arm and dragged him back onstage just as the commercial ended.

Without another word, we all stood up—Gram, Mom, Travis, Nick, and me. Over the mic, I heard the King explain that the Last Insult Standing, Mike or Sharon, would win an all-inclusive cruise to the Bahamas.

We were moving toward the exit when I heard Nick's and my name called out from the stage.

Kirby the Insult King said, "And audience favorites Cassie and Nick will be joining me in my performances on our Celebrity Cruise!"

FROM: MARTIN SMIRNOFF, PRODUCER OF *THE HOUR OF INSULT*
ABOARD THE GOOD SHIP *BEL*
TO: SERINA MADISON,
CASTING DIRECTOR OF *THE HOUR OF INSULT*

Serina, the Christmas Celebrity Cruise is a big hit, thanks in no small part to the two kids. They're working as a team, reminiscent of vaudeville. Not exactly insults, but it's hot. Here's a sample:

Nick: When we boarded this ship, we were hungry.

Cassie: And now we're just fed up.

The King: Easy, you two. I'm not myself today.

Nick: We know. We noticed the improvement right away.

Cassie: Mr. Kirby, thanks for joining us. We've been waiting all day for the pleasure of your company.

Nick: Actually, we're still waiting for that.

The King: You are downright insulting!

Cassie: I know you are, but what am I?

Nick: I'm rubber, and you're glue.

Cassie and Nick: Whatever you say bounces off me and sticks to you!

The King (acting angry): I don't need this. I've got my own TV show.

Cassie: Well, King Kirby, I'd like to say that I don't think your TV show is lousy. But what's my opinion, next to the thousands of others who disagree with me? (She turns to Nick.) As for you, Nick . . . you are fabonomous.

Nick (grinning): Cassie, put a sock in it.

I think we should have them on the show next year.

Marty the Smarty

Jen Callahan
Aboard the Good Ship Bel

Dear Pastor Mike,

Merry Christmas! Here we are, all of us, guests on the Celebrity Cruise. I still can't believe we're all here. Together. I never really thanked you for the visits with my daughter while I was away. Cassie has grown up so much—but not too much.

Thank you for what turned out to be a wedding none of us will ever forget, which is, I suppose, a good thing. I hope nobody really minded having a dog as flower girl and kids as maid of honor and best man. And I hope you were able to get Julie's vomit out of the new carpet. She just couldn't help it. You might try using a spatula, then sprinkling baking soda, followed by cornstarch. The remainder should come out with warm water and a rag.

We are having the time of our lives on our honeymoon. So are Cassie and Nick and Julie and Mom.

Thanks again!
Jen

Emma Hendren
Somewhere in the middle of the ocean on Christmas

Dear Pastor Mike,

Pray for me! The ocean is rough, and I'm seasick. But our family is together at last. You'll be seeing us in our family pew when we return (12th row, left side—don't let the Adams family try to slip in there while we're on the cruise).

Nauseatedly (as Cassie would write),

Emma

Travis Barton
Aboard the Bel

Hi, Dad,

Jen and I and the kids are having a great time. Wish you were here! But at least you made it for the wedding, right? Thanks for staying late and helping with cleanup. Almost everyone was a good sport, don't you think?

We miss you, but I know you'd regret missing that gin rummy tournament at the retirement home. Hope you remembered to go downstairs for it. I'm sure you'll hold on to your championship title. This family seems to have a lot of champs lately! And as Mark Twain said, "History may not repeat itself. But it does rhyme a lot." 175

Love,
Travis

Julie Barton
(as dictated to Cassie)
On a big ship

Dear Kirby the Dog,

All of my whole entire family on this boat is sitting in these lawn chairs on the deck and writing postcards to friends and relatives. Since everybody I might want to write is here, except for Grandad, and I see that Dad is writing him, I am writing you.

I really, really, really miss you, Kirby! As soon as I saw this funny postcard with the dog on it, I thought of you, and I thought you'd like it. Don't eat it, okay?

I can't wait to swing with you and maybe have you sleep on my bed! Cassie says she'd be fine with that idea. I am so thankful that things have worked out for Dad and Jen. We have our family back! And you are part of that family!

See you soon and forever!

Love,
Julie

Kirby the Insult King
Christmas Celebrity Cruise
To: All cast and crew of <u>The Hour of Insult</u>

Did you see those ratings? <u>The Last Insult Standing</u>
went through the roof!
Now leave me alone. I'm on vacation.

Signed,
The King

Nick Barton
Cruise Ship, the Bel

Dear Mom, wherever you are,

Merry Christmas! I am on a big family cruise with
my new big family. We're all super happy, but
it made me think about you. I hope wherever
you are, you're happy. I am sorry you aren't
still part of our family. (Although that probably
wouldn't have worked for Jen, Cassie's mom. She
is very nice and understanding, but not THAT
understanding!)
    Even though I may never see you again, it
would be nice to know that you know Julie and
me are doing fine. Great, in fact! AND I have a
new sister, Cassie! And a dog named Kirby.
    I have never seen Dad so happy. He is not even
a tiny bit grumpy.

Love,
Nick

Cassie Callahan
Aboard the Bel Celebrity Cruise ship
(from "Beleidigung," German for "insult")
Way out in the ocean on your birthday

Dear Jesus,

Well, you did it! Travis and Mom are not just back together. They're married! I don't even care about losing that contest, and neither does Nick. We are exactly where we wanted to be. (And you knew all along, didn't you?)

We really are one big, happy family, and we could not have done it without you. Thank you for letting me ask and ask and knock and seek a million times!

Thanks for your letters and the other stuff in the Bible. I will never forget that one in Colossians, about letting my conversation be gracious so that I will have the right response for everyone.

I've read about you being in those fishing boats and storms at sea and how you walked on water. I'm not going to try any of that. We are all just sitting on the deck of the cruise ship, our lawn chairs shoved close together, while sunlight sparkles the water and the sun sinks into it.

I'm just sayin' . . .

It sure feels like happily ever after.

Love,
Cassie

Acknowledgments

I love my Tyndale team, who work together to make me better than I am. Thanks to Linda Howard, associate publisher, children and youth, for loving to brainstorm ideas and then turning those ideas into realities. Stephanie Riche, senior editor, thank you for your encouragement, wisdom, and friendship. Jackie Nuñez, art director, thanks for sharing your creativity, talents, and artistic gifts with me. And I'm so grateful for Sarah Rubio, my editor, who in addition to her profound skills and keen perception, is a joy to work with. Thanks also to Alyssa Anderson, Brittany Bergman, Nancy Clausen, Raquel Corbin, Jesse Doogan, Kristi Gravemann, Tim Wolf, Stephanie Brockway, Lisanne Kaufmann, Elizabeth Kletzing, and Sheila Urban.

Eternal thanks to my Katy, whose sweet, Julie-like spirit rises above obstacles to touch everyone she meets, leaving us all better people. I can't leave out my Cassie, Ellie, and Maddie, who provide me with endless inspiration.

Finally, I couldn't do anything without my talented and loving husband—my first reader, my constant hero, and the love of my life.

About the Author

DANDI DALEY MACKALL is the award-winning author of over 450 books for children and adults. She visits countless schools, conducts writing assemblies and workshops across the United States, and presents keynote addresses at conferences and young author events. She is also a frequent guest on radio talk shows and has made dozens of appearances on TV. She has won several awards for her writing, including the Helen Keating Ott Award for Contributions to Children's Literature, the Edgar Award, the Christian Children's Book of the Year Award and is a two-time Mom's Choice Award winner.

Dandi writes from rural Ohio, where she lives with her husband, Joe, their three children, and their horses, dogs, and cats. Visit her at DandiBooks.com.

This isn't about me. The story, I mean. So already you got a ~~resort~~ reason to hang it up. At least that's what Mrs. Smith, my teacher, says.

BUT THE STORY *IS* ABOUT TEN-YEAR-OLD LANEY GRAFTON and the new girl in her class—Lara Phelps—whom everyone bullies from the minute she shows up. But instead of acting the way a bullied kid normally acts, this new girl returns kindness for a meanness that intensifies—until nobody remains unchanged, not even the reader.